CW01663852

# THE GREATEST DEPARTURE

*- SECOND MOVIE -*

**Erens Ludik**

Copyright © 2023 *Erens Ludik*
All Rights Reserved

# Dedication

First of all, I want to thank Abba Father God and His Son, Jesus Christ, for His goodness to me. Also, thanks to the precious Holy Spirit, the constant Helper in my heart and thought processes.

Thirdly, I want to thank both my parents, Hennie and Anita, who taught me positive lessons in life. As my father passed away in 1994, my mother's constant help through thick and thin was and is still outstanding. Also, respect to my stepfather, John Hoskins, for his great wisdom and support over the years.

Fourthly, to my precious children Christian, Jessica and Christel. May you fulfil your destiny in God.

Lastly, to my 2 brothers, Jacques and Hein. I am happy to have two great brothers, but I am also happy that I am the youngest. 😊

# Acknowledgements

This is the second movie script out of the Trilogy series, and it is important to acknowledge that without the Trinity of God, all this would not be possible. All glory must go to the Father, The Son and the Holy Spirit, the Three in One!!!

As the idea unfolded and was put into writing, I have some important people to thank who played a pivotal role in helping me through my exciting journey in writing the storyline.

First of all, my mother, Anita Ludik-Hoskins, who helped me with the correct grammar. She was always there along the road, faithfully helping as the script developed.

Secondly, Dr Andrew McDonald. A very good friend with a great sense of humour. Many of the funny scenes in the script have to do with his input. He was also instrumental in editing the script. A true friend!

Thirdly, Stella Heyns who helped polish this initial rough diamond of a script into an eternal shining bright diamond. Her talent speaks for itself, and she played an extremely important role bringing class to the script. I will be forever grateful for that!

# About the Author

Erens Ludik, an entrepreneur with a wealth of business experience, has a passionate heart for God and His people. He is a great encourager who aims to help people find their true destiny on earth. He has written an Epic Trilogy about the End Times in a movie script format. It's full of romance, drama, action and unveiling of the End with great accuracy.

***Contact Erens Ludik***

Website: https://erensludikmovies.com/

Email: info@erensludikmovies.com

*(Matthew, the disciple of Jesus (formerly a tax collector), is writing with an ink feather pen. A voice audibly read it while he is writing Matthew, 24:31)*

"And He will send His angels with a great sound of a trumpet, and they will gather together His elect from the four winds, from one end of heaven to the other".

## *Next Scene*

## *A Bus scene*

*A guy is standing at a bus stop next to Bath Street at Portobello beach in Edinburgh, Scotland. A red bus, number 66, is arriving, and as he gets onto the bus, the bus disappears, and the guy finds himself walking in Adderley Street, Cape Town, with Table Mountain in the background.*

***Next Scene***

*Jodhi and Helen are both sitting at a table at Durbanville Hills Wine farm. They have a great view on the vineyard as well as on Table Mountain. They are having a glass of red wine together.*

**JODHI**

*(Looking over the vineyards)* It's time, Helen! God's harvest is ready. This is the time we all have been waiting for.
"The Great Tribulation"

*(clinks glasses)*

***(Song plays "Days of Elijah" by Robin Mark.)***

**HELEN**

It's like you said, God has kept his best wine for last! It's like the Wedding Feast scene in John 2 in the Bible. Our wedding was a foretaste of that.

(*Helen is smiling.)*

**JODHI**

It sure was!

(*Jodhi gives Helen a kiss.)*

Yeah, especially if you think about those six jars of water that Jesus turned into the best wine...
We know that those six jars represent the 6000 years of Mankind getting ready for Jesus' Millennial reign of 1000 years on earth.
But not yet!
We have to go through these last 42 months, then everything will be done as He has promised and will come into fulfilment.

**HELEN**

42 months... that is more than 3 years.
Okay, tell me more – explain to me in plain English what it all means?

**JODHI**

Well, for starters, we are about to see the greatest work of God on this planet.

**HELEN**

How come?

**JODHI**

It is actually incredibly exciting. The whole of Heaven is watching – all the great Saints in the Bible – the whole host of Saints are looking at us in great expectation.
Helen, we are part of something incredible that's about to happen. The great acts of God are to be displayed right now.

**HELEN**

This is why we came to Cape Town, right?

**JODHI**

Sure, this is it. It's Revelation 12:6

**HELEN**

What does it say?

**JODHI**

*(Jodhi is reading Revelation 12:6)*

"Then the woman fled into the wilderness, where she has a place prepared by God, that they should feed her there one thousand two hundred and sixty days."

**HELEN**

Who is the woman?

**JODHI**

The woman is God's people who obeyed Him and have been prepared for the Great Tribulation. Let me read to you Revelation 12:14. "But the woman was given two wings of a great eagle, that she might fly into the wilderness to her place, where she is nourished for a time and times and half a time, from the presence of the serpent."

**HELEN**

I get it! The great eagle represents aeroplanes to take His people to a place of safety. That's why we have started the Saints 888 Airline business.

**JODHI**

Hallelujah! God has given me a clever wife.

*(Jodhi is smiling at Helen. They kiss each other.)*

*Next Scene*

*(Jodhi and Helen are watching at the venue the news on CNN. It shows an outbreak of war in Israel. Lots of Jews are fleeing for their lives. War has broken out with Syria and all neighbouring countries in the Middle East are involved.)*

**HELEN**

Wow, things are getting serious. Things are getting real, real fast.

**JODHI**

Yeah, the time has come. It's a good thing we have a meeting with Ernst and Emma tomorrow morning.

**HELEN**

Shouldn't we go home now? It's getting late?

*Next Scene*

**JODHI**

Let's go.

*(It's the next morning. Jodhi and Helen are driving to Cape Town International Airport for the meeting with Ernst and Emma.)*

***('Exodus' by Bob Marley** is playing on the radio while driving to the airport.)*

*(Jodhi and Helen park the car at the airport, and they head into the meeting with Ernst and Emma.)*

**JODHI**

Good morning guys.

**ERNST**

Hi, good to see you. Have you seen the breaking news?

*(Ernst is pointing them to the CNN Channel on the TV Screen in the board room.)*

**JODHI**

We sure have, and now you can see how important it was to set up an airline for God's purposes!

**ERNST**

Sure! We are such an unlikely army, but our Emma is doing such a great job of organising the transport from China. We are getting a lot more Saint 888 Airbuses from the plant in Shanghai.

**JODHI**

Yeah, we will be needing them. We have 153 international airports to serve.

**HELEN**

Cape Town airport is going to be incredibly busy. It's our main hub in Southern Africa.

**EMMA**

You are right. And we have put the logistics in place in order to support that.

**JODHI**

That's very good because time is of the essence.

*(A scene on CNN shows the two witnesses standing at the Wailing Wall in Jerusalem. They are warning people to follow Christ only and not to give in to the New World System. They are directing people to go to Southern Africa, where a place is prepared for them.)*

**HELEN**

Are these the two witnesses that were foretold in Revelation?

**JODHI**

Yes, it's all in Revelation 11, and it's coming into fulfilment right here, right now.

***Scene flash***
***Revelation 11:4-6***

*(Computer Generated Imagery and an audible voice reading it)*

"These are the two olive trees and the two lampstands standing before the God of the earth. And if anyone wants to harm them, fire proceeds from their mouth and devours their enemies.
And if anyone wants to harm them, he must be killed in this manner. These have power to shut heaven so that no rain falls in the days of their prophecy; and they have power over waters to turn them to blood, and to strike the earth with all plagues, as often as they desire".

**EMMA**

So, everything is already foretold about what is going to happen?

**JODHI**

Sure thing and the best part of it is that we are chosen to live during this time!

**EMMA**

Wow, I see a lot of bookings are coming in.

*(Referring to the system on her laptop)*

We need to employ more people.

**ERNST**

That's no problem. I will get more in a flash. You know I am Sonic.

(*Everyone is laughing.)*

**JODHI**

Well, we have to leave now. I think if we see each other at 8 am sharp tomorrow that would be good.

**ERNST**

That's perfect.

*(Jodhi and Helen are driving to their home in Durbanville. The* ***Song of Bob Marley*** *is playing on the radio* ***"Don't worry about a thing."*** *They go to bed. Jodhi awakes at 3 in the morning.)*

*(Jesus appears to him.)*

**JESUS**

Jodhi, My beloved servant. I want you to contact my two witnesses. They have to come to Cape Town. You have to book them on one of the private jets with their wives. I will direct them to go to Tel Aviv airport to get a flight on your airline to Cape Town, my chosen City for this time.

*(Jesus disappears.)*

***Scene in Jerusalem***

*(Scene of the two witnesses, Boaz and Jachin, talking to each other. They are in the lounge of the King David Hotel. Boaz is telling Jachin that he had a dream about them going to Cape Town on Saints 888 Airline.)*

**JACHIN**

*(Boaz enters the lounge of the King David Hotel in Jerusalem. Jachin is sitting down and having a coffee. Boaz is joining him.)*

Shalom, Boaz.

**BOAZ**

Shalom, my good friend.

**JACHIN**

Did you have a good sleep?

**BOAZ**

I haven't really slept at all, but I had a visitation from Yeshua.

**JACHIN**

Really?

**BOAZ**

He told me we should fly with Rachel and Suyin to Cape Town International Airport. He has work for us to do there.

**JACHIN**

I always knew Cape Town was going to be important at this time. That’s why we are directing the people to go to Southern Africa. So when should we go?

**BOAZ**

Now, quickly. I will call Saints 888 Airline to find out when the first available booking is that they can give us.

**JACHIN**

Ok yeah, but we have to let the women know too.

**BOAZ**

Sure.

*(Boaz is calling the Airline.)*

*Next Scene*

*In the meantime, all over the world, TV channels in different countries have breaking news about what is happening across the world. Scenes follow some people's reactions to the events.*

*The first scene is of a man sitting in a bar in Dallas, Texas, with two girls dressed as Dallas Cowboys (American football team) cheerleaders on both sides next to him.* ***OMI – Cheerleader song " by Felix Jaehn Remix plays****. One girl is blonde, and the other girl is a brunette. Johnny is kissing both of the 2 girls. A friend of his is tapping him on his back. His friend Jack is telling him to look at MSNBC news on the TV screen in the bar. It's breaking news of the scenes unfolding in Jerusalem. Riots are happening all over in Jerusalem.)*

**JACK**

Daaaaaamn, Johnny, check this out!

*(Pointing to the TV behind the bar – scenes from MSNBC news.)*

**JOHNNY**

Jack, you worry too much. Relax. Get yourself another Jack!

*(referring to Jack Daniels whiskey)*

*(Chuckles at his own lame joke.)*

**JACK**

Johnny, I tell you, this is serious.

**JOHNNY**

Don't worry, JACKY BOY! Look at us - we are here in a nice bar in Dallas with 2 beautiful girls. We are living life. Let the Jerusalem problems stay in Jerusalem. Let them sort out their own problems.
Let our biggest problems tonight be to decide what to drink or which of these lovely ladies we smile at next. I tell you - it's probably all fake news anyway. Conspiracy theory on acid, if you ask me.
What is serious, Jacky Boy, is that you need to get a grip.

*Next Scene*

*(Another scene occurs in Rio De Janeiro, Brazil. A guy named Rodriquez is sitting in a beach bar in Rio de Janeiro with Christ The Redeemer statue on Mount Corcovado in the background view. Breaking news appears on the TV screen, interrupting a Brazil football game.* ***"We are One Ole Ola" football song*** *is playing in the background.)*

**RODRIQUEZ**

What is this crap about? How can they interrupt our game?
E ai bastardos. (Subtitles: Oh, Bastards!)

**WAITRESS SALMA**

Rodriquez, this is bigger news than any football game. Remember that God is bigger than man's football.

*(On TV, the Pope is speaking from the Vatican. He is pronouncing that all religions should unite in this time of crisis. He says we are all one world and should embrace a One World Religion.)*

**RODRIQUEZ**

What is the pope speaking about? I'd rather drink 55 Tequila shots before I embrace a One World Religion.

**WAITRESS SALMA**

Nothing new there then; you are already drinking that amount of Tequila shots.

*(Salma is laughing.)*

**RODRIQUEZ**

I know. Give me a few more. I need it after listening to this rubbish.

*Next Scene*

*( Next Scene is in the Venetian Casino in Macau, China. Mr Chan, a billionaire in China, is playing Black Jack.)*

***The song "Money, Money, Money" by Abba plays in the background.***

**DEALER AT THE BLACK JACK TABLE**

Good day Mr Chan. I see you are back again. Such a pleasure.

**MR CHAN**

Yeah, Jack is back to deal with Black Jack. (*Both laugh.)*

*(Breaking news on the TV Screen. An announcement out of the United Nations building is made. The Secretary-General of the United Nations is introducing to the world a new currency and a chip on the forehead or on the hand for everyone to buy and sell.)*

**MR CHAN**

*(Laughs)*

Fools. They can forget about it.
I would rather put all my money on chips right here!

**DEALER AT THE BLACK JACK TABLE**

Knowing you, Mr Chan, you will probably do that. If anyone can, Mr Chan can.

*(The dealer is laughing.)*

**MR CHAN**

You bet I will. Give me a Montecristo cigar, and I will say that again. Let them stick it in their pipe and smoke it!

***Scene in Kingston, Jamaica***

*(Bobby is speaking to his good old friend Eric. They are sitting outside having a ganja smoke. They have the jukebox out.* ***The song plays by UB40, "Kingston Town".)***

**BOBBY**

You know what, Eric, my friend? It's our time; our time has come.

**ERIC**

What do you mean, Bobby?

**BOBBY**

My mother told me when I was a child that I had a great destiny. I think this is it unfolding.

**ERIC**

What makes you say that?

**BOBBY**

I listened to the news yesterday. It's time, brother.

**ERIC**

For what?

**BOBBY**

A real trip to Africa. Bob Marley, Boney M, UB40 and the whole gang they all like our Kingston town. Bob had it right; it was time for Exodus.

**ERIC**

I know Bob Marley is your favourite. You told me once your mother named you after him.

**BOBBY**

Yeah, man. I understand him now. He was singing about Exodus.

**ERIC**

Yeah, I don't really understand that song. That was a long time ago when Moses took the Israelites out of Egypt.

**BOBBY**

Yeah, brother, but he was singing about something in the future.

**ERIC**

Like what?

**BOBBY**

Like now, you know he liked Haile Selassie a lot.

**ERIC**

Yeah, I know.

**BOBBY**

It's because Haile Selassie was from the Tribe of Judah. He came from a long family line from King Solomon.

**ERIC**

You mean he is part of the Royal family of Israel?

**BOBBY**

Yeah, man. King Solomon married the Queen of Sheba of Ethiopia. He is part of the family.

**ERIC**

I get you, brother. Let's smoke another ganja.

**BOBBY**

Yeah, why not? I tell you, I was listening yesterday evening to the news on TV. There were these two guys in Jerusalem...

I am telling you, man...Those 2 are like the pillars of Solomon's temple. They are talking about God. In front of the whole world.

People are staring. Cameras and phones taking videos.
And you know what, man? No one can touch them. They are untouchable.

**ERIC**

Yeah, man, the untouchables.

***Scene back in Jerusalem***

*Boaz and Jachin and their wives are all leaving the King David Hotel in Jerusalem. They are getting into a taxi. Boaz and Jachin are speaking to the taxi driver.*

**BOAZ**

Thanks for being on time.

**TAXI DRIVER PHILIP**

No worries, it's my job.

**BOAZ**

Where is that accent from?

**TAXI DRIVER PHILIP**

I was born in Ethiopia, but my dad was originally from Jamaica.

**BOAZ**

That's fab. We are on our way to Cape Town, South Africa.

**TAXI DRIVER PHILIP**

Wow, that's amazing. My mother got baptized there. That's why she called me after Philip the Evangelist in the bible.

**JACHIN**

That's very interesting.

**TAXI DRIVER PHILIP**

Yea, she went to a Christian Crusade held by Reinhardt Bonke. Do you know him?

**BOAZ**

Of course. He was instrumental in the Evangelism of Africa. Like David Livingstone, the great pioneer missionary for Africa.

**TAXI DRIVER PHILIP**

Wow, so you wise guys are also Christians?

**BOAZ**

Yeah. We love Jesus.

**TAXI DRIVER PHILIP**

That's amazing. When I woke up today, I felt this was going to be a great day!

**BOAZ**

Well, we are also happy about today.

**TAXI DRIVER PHILIP**

May I ask what you guys are doing?

**BOAZ**

We are working for our King.

**TAXI DRIVER PHILIP**

Gosh. I have picked up royalty?

**BOAZ**

*(Boaz is laughing.)* We are not royalty, just serving our King.

**TAXI DRIVER PHILIP**

Forgive me. May I ask you another question?

**BOAZ**

Of course.

**TAXI DRIVER PHILIP**

Which King are you serving? The King of Jordan?

**JACHIN**

*(Jachin is laughing.)* No, our King is the same king you are serving.

**TAXI DRIVER PHILIP**

Ahh, I get you! You are talking about Jesus. You are right; we are all His servants.

**BOAZ**

It looks like we are here. I wish you God's grace, my friend.

**TAXI DRIVER PHILIP**

Thank you, Sir. Have a safe flight to South Africa.

**BOAZ**

Don't worry, my friend; God controls the skies. (*Boaz is smiling.)*

***Next Scene***

*(Boaz and Jachin and their wives are leaving the taxi. They board a private jet and fly to Cape Town. Arriving at Cape Town International Airport, they meet Jodhi and Helen.)*

**JODHI**

Good day. I am Mr Livingstone.

**BOAZ**

A pleasure to meet you, Mr Livingstone. Thanks for organising our flight.

**JODHI**

The privilege is mine.

**BOAZ**

This is my wife Rachel, Jachin and his wife Suyin.

**JODHI**

Great to eventually meet you guys. This is my wife, Helen.

*(They all greet with a handshake and take a minibus to the 12 Apostles Hotel.)*

*(They arrive at the 12 Apostles hotel and have lunch together.)*

**BOAZ**

This is a lovely place with awesome sea views.

**JODHI**

Yeah. I chose this place to get engaged to Helen.

**BOAZ**

What an inspiring choice.

**RACHEL**

I am always interested in love stories. So, tell us, how did you guys meet?

**JODHI**

I will let Helen tell the story. Women are so much better at telling love stories. (*They are all laughing.)*

**HELEN**

Well, Jodhi is actually the real hero of the day we met. I was out with my friend in San Francisco. We were at the Candy Bar. We were sitting outside, and a stranger tried to steal my handbag. He came from behind and grabbed my handbag, and ran off. Jodhi ran after him and tackled him in the street. The handbag fell on the street, and the stranger ran off, but Jodhi got my handbag back. From then on, he became my hero.

(*Helen is blushing.)*

**RACHEL**

Ahw! what a nice start. (*All of them are smiling.)*

**HELEN**

Yeah, to repay the favour, I invited him to a BBQ at our family home. After meeting the family, we became inseparable, and the rest is history.

**SUYIN**

That's a beautiful story.

**JODHI**

Thanks. Well, Suyin, you look as if you are from the Far East. Which country are you originally from?

**SUYIN**

I am originally from Hong Kong.

**JODHI**

That's interesting. I have a friend called Ernst. His wife is originally from Hong Kong before she moved to London. Maybe it's a good idea to introduce her to you.

**SUYIN**

It would be lovely to speak to someone from back home!

**JODHI**

Yeah, she is helping us with the logistics of our Airbus plant in Shanghai.

**BOAZ**

We can't wait to hear about these Airbuses and your plans, Brother! We have much to discuss. It brings me to the mission and why we are here.

**JODHI**

We are all ears.

**BOAZ**

We feel like Cape Town is a chosen city for this time. When I read Psalm 125:1, the Lord was speaking with me about Table Mountain.

He sees Table Mountain like He sees Mount Zion. It's no coincidence that this mountain is called the 12 Apostles. It ties in with Revelation 14, where God's saints are on Mount Zion. Although the real Mount Zion is in Jerusalem, we feel God has chosen Cape Town as headquarters for His saints in this hour.

**JACHIN**

Yeah, we feel like the Lord is calling all His servants to Southern Africa in these coming 42 months.

**JODHI**

That's amazing. It's the same vision I got.

**JACHIN**

Well, it looks like God has put us together for such a time like this.

**SUYIN**

It's exciting. So, what is the next step?

**JODHI**

Well, the Great Tribulation is about to start, so now we will be very busy locating God saints in different locations from Cape Town up to Southern Ethiopia.

**HELEN**

Yeah. What is that lake that you have mentioned before in Ethiopia?

**JODHI**

Lake Tana. It is the largest lake in Ethiopia and the source of the Blue Nile.

**HELEN**

And you have also mentioned Lake Victoria, the source of the White Nile.

**JODHI**

That's right. Lake Victoria was found by the English Explorer John Hanning Speke from the Tanzanian side.

**HELEN**

What makes these 2 lakes so important?

**JODHI**

Well, they are pointers. They are clues for us to understand the time we live in. As Zephaniah 3:10 says, "From beyond the rivers of Ethiopia, My worshippers, the daughter of my dispersed ones, will bring My offering."

**BOAZ**

You mean that ties in with the 144,000 in the Book of Revelation.

**JODHI**

That's correct. It's just a symbolic number. It includes all God's saints who follow the Lamb.

**JACHIN**

So, what's the symbolic meaning of the 144,000?

**JODHI**

The 144,000 refers to a remnant that is described in symbolic terms. The number "12" in the Bible is a symbol of authority. 12 tribes of Israel, 12 disciples, etc. Therefore 12x12 = 144. The thousand represent the fullness of quantity.

**RACHEL**

So, what you are saying is that God has prepared Southern Africa to be a place of Safety for His Saints. That's why Boaz and Jachin were directing the people at the Western Wall in Jerusalem to Southern Africa.

**JODHI**

Exactly.

**BOAZ**

It all makes sense now. That's why God told us to come here.

**JODHI**

Yes, so today we will give you some time on your own to relax. Then tomorrow morning let's say we meet at 11. I will bring my friend Ernst and his wife Emma so that you can meet them too.

**BOAZ**

Sounds great.

*Next Scene*

*(It's the next day, and they meet all on the balcony of the 12 Apostles Hotel. They are having a cup of tea.)*

**JODHI**

It's a beautiful morning. Let's sit outside.

**EMMA**

Yeah, I love the sea here. It reminds me of my time in Hong Kong. We loved to go out on the boat over weekends.

**SUYIN**

We did the same it was loads of fun. We would even go diving in the sea.

**JODHI**

That reminds me. We met a lady called Ann in Rome. She is helping us with an online digital bank for God's saints. She loves diving too.

**SUYIN**

Where is she originally from?

**JODHI**

She is from Rome but originally China. She is helping us with the bank here in Cape Town.

**HELEN**

Her dad is from Italy, but her mum is from China. I should organise a ladies outing between us one day. (*Helen is smiling.)*

**EMMA**

That will be fun. She would love to make new friends.

**RACHEL**

Good idea... It looks like we are getting a nice gang together. (*Rachel is smiling.)*

**JODHI**

Well, if you ladies can have a day out, I am sure our guys can hang out for a day as well.

*(chuckle)*

Then we can have a nice Braai/BBQ by the pool for the boys.

**BOAZ**

That sounds like a great plan; I haven't had a BBQ for a long time.

**JODHI**

I'll make sure you get plenty of that here, don't worry! (*Jodhi is laughing.)*

**HELEN**

It's such a beautiful day, Jodhi! Maybe our guests can take the day off and relax at the beach...? Or explore a bit?

**JODHI**

I think that's a great idea! It's such a bright sunny day. The beach will be brilliant. Tomorrow morning, we can have a board meeting at our offices. I have invited Ann to join us too.

**BOAZ**

Good idea.

**JODHI**

I will organise our driver to pick you guys up tomorrow at 10 am for the meeting.

**JACHIN**

Cool.

*(They say goodbye. It's the next day. Everyone is at the meeting. They plan a schedule for the month.)*

**JODHI**

So great that we have the team together. I want to introduce you to Ann. Everybody, this is Ann.

*(They all greet Ann.)*

**JODHI**

Helen and I had an unusual way of meeting her. We met her at the Spanish steps in Rome. The Lord directed me to speak to her. She has a special task in what we are doing together. We set up a digital online bank for His Saints at this time.
It will help us to buy and sell independently from the World System, where one has to get the chip introduced by the United Nations to buy and sell.

**BOAZ**

Wow, that's a perfect idea. It sounds like the Lord. Ann, we are happy to meet you.

**ANN**

It's a pleasure. I am happy to meet you guys. It just felt right to come with Helen and Jodhi to Cape Town to start this fightback.

**RACHEL**

Yeah, I understand that feeling. When Boaz and I met Suyin and Jachin, we had that same feeling. We knew it was destiny to meet. Destiny is the thing.

**ANN**

That's interesting. How did the 4 of you meet?

**RACHEL**

Well, we were at a Church conference in Singapore. I sat next to Suyin, and we became good friends from there on.

**SUYIN**

Yes, then we introduced our husbands to each other and from then on, it was fireworks between the 4 of us.

**ANN**

So, where are you originally from?

**SUYIN**

Well, Jachin is from Singapore, and I am from Hong Kong originally.

**RACHEL**

And we are from LA. I grew up in Israel before I moved to LA.

**JODHI**

Which part of Israel are you originally from?

**RACHEL**

I was born in Jaffa and grew up in Tel Aviv.

**JODHI**

That's very interesting. Jaffa is the place where Saint Peter got the vision that the gospel is open to the whole world.

**RACHEL**

That's right.

**JODHI**

Have you ever been to the sea of Galilea?

**RACHEL**

Yes, many times as a child.

**JODHI**

The story that fascinates me a lot in the gospel of John is the miracle of catching 153 large fish. I believe there was a meaning to it. Why it was 153?

**BOAZ**

What would be the meaning?

**JODHI**

I believe that 153 nations will be open to the gospel in The Great Tribulation as it is the last harvest before the coming of the Lord. The emphasis on large fish is because it's a great harvest of souls for His Kingdom.

**JACHIN**

That's an interesting point.

**JODHI**

I have found another passage in the Bible that refers to the number 153. It's in 2 Kings 1 when Elijah confronted 3 groups of 50 men, with each group having a captain, so in total, thus the number 153.
He challenges them on Mount Carmel, telling them that fire will come down from heaven and consume them if he is a man of God. So, it happened then.

**JACHIN**

I know that story very well. The Lord is still speaking with Boaz and me about it. You have some good revelation there.

**JODHI**

Yeah, ironically, I was a former pastor at Carmel-by- the-Sea in California. It was called after the Carmelites, formally known as the Order of the Brothers of the Blessed Virgin Mary of Mount Carmel.

**BOAZ**

I like you already, Jodhi. You have interesting stories.

**JODHI**

I like you too. (*Jodhi is laughing.*) Wait till we have a BBQ at Ernst place. He has a nice firepit, and we can share a lot of stories.

**ERNST**

That sounds like a brilliant idea. What about this Friday night?

**JODHI**

Is everyone ok with that? (*Everyone is saying yes.)*

*Next Scene*

*(It's Friday night, and the whole group is at Ernst's place. The men are standing around the fire and are chatting.)*

**BOAZ**

I like your place, Ernst. This is so relaxing now.

**ERNST**

Yeah, Jodhi and I do a lot of BBQs here. We call it a "braai". (Subtitles: Barbeque)

**BOAZ**

I see. Jodhi has told me in the car. You are like Father Abraham of old. He must have done a lot of BBQs at his tent back in his day. (*Everyone is laughing.)*

**JODHI**

So, Ernst, I see you have bought us a lot of fish.

**ERNST**

Yeah, I thought, for a change, let's do a fish braai.

**JODHI**

Good idea.

*Scene in The Kitchen with The Women*

**RACHEL**

So, who's this lovely sweety?

**EMMA**

She is our daughter Mulan.

**RACHEL**

What a beautiful girl.

**SUYIN**

Yes, I like the name. So, you must have called her after Mulan, the Chinese girl warrior?

**EMMA**

Yes indeed.

**SUYIN**

We need a lot of woman warriors like Mulan in these times. Women are the power behind the throne. (*Suyin is smiling.)*

**RACHEL**

For sure. So, tell me, Helen. How did you guys eventually come over to South Africa?

**HELEN**

Well, it all started in New York. We were there together for a break. Jodhi wanted to visit his friend on Staten Island, and I was going to stay at the hotel. The taxi he took was in a crash on the way to his friend's.

**RACHEL**

Oh, my word. What happened then?

**HELEN**

Well, they went to Mount Sinai Hospital. The taxi driver was ok, but Jodhi had to get surgery on his left arm.

**SUYIN**

Is his arm better?

**HELEN**

Kind of. He went for a few physio sessions but still has some pain.

**SUYIN**

Has he tried acupuncture before?

**HELEN**

No. Is it good?

**SUYIN**

Yeah, it helped me. I did some heavy lifting, and my arm got badly hurt.
A friend of mine advised me to go for acupuncture.

**HELEN**

Do you have any more pain?

**SUYIN**

No, the pain is gone.

**HELEN**

That's fantastic news. Maybe that is what Jodhi should do.

**EMMA**

Yeah, I think so too. I have a friend that knows a good Chinese specialist in Acupuncture. I will get the contact number then you can make an appointment with them.

**HELEN**

Thanks. That's a good idea.

**EMMA**

Shall we join the men outside?

**RACHEL**

Yeah, let's see what they are up to. (*The women are smiling.)*

*Next Scene*

*(They are all sitting around the fire pit and having a glass of wine.)*

**BOAZ**

This South African wine is nice. What is this one called?

**JODHI**

It's a Sauvignon Blanc from Durbanville Hills farm.

**BOAZ**

It tastes refreshing. Here's to friends.

**JODHI**

Cheers to us! *(They all clink glasses.)*

**ERNST**

This wine is popular worldwide. They export a lot of good wine from Durbanville Hills farm.

**BOAZ**

So why is South African wine so good?

**ERNST**

It's because our climate is perfect for wine, and we are positioned close to the sea. Another important factor was that the Huguenots from France started the wine industry in South Africa. They were farmers in France and very familiar with wine growing. There is a whole town here called Franschhoek. It means French corner in Afrikaans.

**BOAZ**

So, the Huguenots were Protestants, right?

**ERNST**

Yes, they had to flee Europe because of the Edict of Nantes, which was revoked in October 1685. That caused the Exodus of Protestants from Europe. It also increased the hostility of Protestant nations bordering France.

**RACHEL**

Sorry for being so ignorant. What was the Edict of Nantes?

**ERNST**

The Edict of Nantes was signed in April 1598 by King Henry IV and granted the Calvinist Protestants of France, also known as Huguenots, substantial rights in the nation, which was, in essence, completely Catholic.

**JACHIN**

So, a lot of the Huguenots ended up in South Africa, right?

**ERNST**

Yes, I am also a Huguenot from my mother's side. Her surname was Retief. Piet Retief is part of our family. He was a leading figure during the Great Trek.

**HELEN**

What was the Great Trek about?

**ERNST**

To answer that question, you first have to understand European history in South Africa. The Dutch East Indian Company was established in 1652 as a halfway station in Cape Town to the Far East. After that, a lot of Europeans followed. The new community that was established consisted mostly of Dutch, Germans, and French.

**JACHIN**

So, before them, who was living in South Africa?

**ERNST**

There were a lot of African Tribes. Different African Tribes migrated from middle Africa to Southern Africa.
Also, in Cape Town, it was mostly the Khoi Khoi people. They were a very peaceful nation. Then you had the Zulus, which became a strong nation in KwaZulu Natal.

**JACHIN**

Yeah, I have heard of them. They had a strong leader called Shaka Zulu.

**ERNST**

Correct. He was the leader who was murdered in 1828 by Dingaan, who was the half-brother of Shaka Zulu. It was before that in 1806 that the English settled in South Africa. They took the colony over from the Dutch. This was when the European pioneers called the "Voortrekkers" wanted their own Freedom. So that's why the Great Trek started in 1835.

**BOAZ**

Is that where your leader Piet Retief comes in?

**ERNST**

You got it, Boaz. He was their leader who would be elected as governor of the Voortrekkers on 17 April 1837.

**BOAZ**

So, Ernst, tell me a bit more about the Airline business.

**ERNST**

Well, we operate with 153 international airports to bring the nations to Southern Africa.

**BOAZ**

So, I presume the 153 international ports are based on the 153 fish that were caught in the Sea of Galilea.

**ERNST**

Correct Boaz! Sharp observation. We have a manufacturing plant for our Airbuses in Shanghai. So, we make sure we have enough planes that we operate with. Emma is in charge of that.

**SUYIN**

That's a big responsibility. Well done, Emma!!

**EMMA**

No pressure. I try. (*Emma is smiling*.)

**RACHEL**

Ann, tell us a bit more about what you are doing.

**ANN**

Well, as you know, I assist Jodhi and Helen in running an online digital bank. Our headquarters are on the Waterfront in Cape Town. We have staff throughout Southern Africa.

**BOAZ**

I understand that you have a lot of Gold in Southern Africa. Do you work with Gold, also?

**ANN**

Yes, that's more Jodhi and Helen's territory.

**JODHI**

Yeah, we secure a lot of gold from Southern Africa for our bank. I also have my son Christian involved, who helps us with the gold and the diamonds. When we do the next BBQ at my place, I will introduce him to you and my daughter Jessica.

**BOAZ**

I am looking forward to that.

**JODHI**

We can do it next weekend.

***Next Scene***

*(It's the next weekend at Jodhi's place. His children, Christian and Jessica, are there and the whole group. They have a spit braai with a big fire pit.)*

**JODHI**

Hi guys, this is Christian and Jessica.

*(They all say hello to them.)*

**BOAZ**

So, Christian, we heard that you are helping your dad in the business.

**CHRISTIAN**

Yes, I am still training, but dad gives me a lot of responsibility.

**BOAZ**

That's good. You know Solomon in the bible? He started young at age 18 to rule affairs. God gave him a lot of wisdom because he asked for that.

**CHRISTIAN**

Yes, I need a lot of wisdom in this business. (*Christian is smiling.)*

**JACHIN**

I am sure you will do well. Whenever God is with you, there is nothing to fear.

**CHRISTIAN**

Thanks.

**JACHIN**

This is your sister?

**CHRISTIAN**

Yes, that's her. (*They all are smiling.)*

**SUYIN**

Jessica, how old are you?

**JESSICA**

I am 14 years old.

**RACHEL**

You are so beautiful. What do you want to do one day?

**JESSICA**

Well, I have 2 dreams. One is to go to space, and the other is the be an actress.

**RACHEL**

I am sure you can do both. You look like a very smart girl.

**JESSICA**

Oh, thank you very much.

**RACHEL**

Well, I hope all your dreams come true.

**JESSICA**

Thank you.

**JODHI**

Ok, guys. Help yourself to drinks. Today we have lamb chops and chicken.

**ANN**

Looking forward to that. I have tasted Jodhi's chicken from a previous BBQ; it's brilliant!

**BOAZ**

Well, 2 great choices. Chicken and lamb are my favourites.

**JODHI**

So, Boaz tell us a bit about you? What prepared you for a time like this?

**BOAZ**

Well, like Jachin, we both received prophetic words about our calling at the same time when we were young. It was just a matter of time before we met each other.

**HELEN**

It's exciting. It feels the same with Jodhi and me. It was just in God's time that we met.

**JACHIN**

Yeah, I also think we all met together at God's *Kairos* (Subtitles: "Divine") time. It's as if God has put a small gang together.

**JODHI**

Yeah, I know it feels like that. What do you see as the next step forward?

**BOAZ**

Well, the first thing God told us was that we were to go to Jerusalem and proclaim His word before the outbreak of the Great Tribulation. The next thing God told us was to come here and meet you guys. So, I guess we are into the third thing soon.

**HELEN**

Can you tell us more about the Anti-Christ?

**BOAZ**

If you read the book of Daniel, chapter 11, you see that the King of the North represents the Antichrist. The King of the North in Daniel's time represented Syria.

**JODHI**

I have read the book of Maccabees. Antiochus IV Epiphanes was a Hellenistic Syrian King. He was the one that attacked Jerusalem and put an idol in the temple.

**JACHIN**

That's correct; that was the time of the Maccabees Revolt and the great miracle of Hanukkah.

**JODHI**

So, if I understand you correctly, both kings were from Syria and lived in different times, but the first one was an archetype or forerunner for the last one to come.

**BOAZ**

Man, Jodhi, I said it before, and I say it again. You are a man after my own heart. You understand these things. (*They all are laughing.)*

**JODHI**

Yeah, man, when I grew up, we lived next to a guy that owned a company called Bright Lights. It must have rubbed off on me. (*Jodhi is smiling.)*

**BOAZ**

Steady now. You still have to use a lot of that bright light. (*Boaz smiling*.)

**JODHI**

So, you reckon that we have the last one here.

**BOAZ**

100%. This is what has happened in Jerusalem in the last couple of weeks.
That's the reason Jachin, and I have been sent to Jerusalem.

**HELEN**

What about the false prophet?

**JACHIN**

Well, you have seen what the Pope has recently announced. He wants to accept all religions and make them a one-world religion. Also, he encourages us to follow the United Nations in introducing a new world order.

**ANN**

I am beginning to understand some of this now. I bet your next mission is going to Rome. (*Ann is smiling.)*

**JACHIN**

I think you have hit the nail right on the head. *(Jachin is smiling.)*

**BOAZ**

Yes, you got it. We are going to Rome.

**HELEN**

As the saying goes, all roads lead to Rome.

**BOAZ**

Tomorrow Rome but after that the 4 corners of the world await.

***Next Scene***

*(Scene of Boaz and Jachin in Rome in front of the St. Peter Basilica preaching the gospel. People by the thousands flock to hear them. They are warning people not to take the mark of the beast.)*

*Next Scene*

*Jodhi is watching CNN on TV showing the 2 witnesses in Rome. He is speaking with his wife, Helen. Christian and Jessica are also sitting in the living room.)*

**JODHI**

It's amazing to see them in Rome. The last time when we saw them on TV in Jerusalem, we didn't know them. Now they are such good friends.

**HELEN**

Yeah, they are such nice people. I think Suyin suggestion to go for acupuncture is a good idea.

**JODHI**

You could follow that up with Emma and book an appointment with her contact.

**HELEN**

Yeah, sure, I will call her now.

*Next Scene*

*(Jodhi is with a Chinese Acupuncture specialist called Hua.)*

**HUA**

So, Emma told me you and your wife are very good friends with her.

**JODHI**

Yes, she is married to my best school friend, Ernst.

**HUA**

Oh, I see. So, how does your arm feel?

**JODHI**

It feels good, but there is still a pain that won't go away.

**HUA**

You're in the right place. We have helped thousands of people, and they are all pain-free today.

**JODHI**

Well, that sounds good to me.

**HUA**

Do you know anything about acupuncture?

**JODHI**

Not really, but I was told it comes from a long history in China.

**HUA**

Yes. The theory of acupuncture tells us that energy flows within the human body, and this energy can be channelled to create balance and health. This energy flow, or life force, is called qi or chi.

**JODHI**

It sounds like Chai in Hebrew, which means living or life.

**HUA**

It's a very similar meaning.

**JODHI**

Yes, the Jewish people will tell you that you should choose life or death, blessing or curse and if you are wise that you should choose Life which is God.

**HUA**

That's interesting.

**JODHI**

I am a Christian. I believe in Jesus. We find true life. Jesus also gives Eternal Life to all who believe in Him.

**HUA**

Chi has a spiritual meaning too. God is the source of life.

**JODHI**

I agree.

**HUA**

Ok, let us start with the session. If you can lie down for me, please.

**JODHI**

Sure.

*(Jodhi is lying down on the bed, and Hua is giving him the treatment. Jodhi's body reacts very well to it. He feels pain leaving his body and feeling refreshed.)*

**HUA**

So, Mr Livingstone, how do you feel?

**JODHI**

I feel very good and very alive indeed. (*Jodhi is smiling.)*

**HUA**

Very good, just like your surname Mr Livingstone. (*Hua is smiling.)*

**JODHI**

Indeed.

**HUA**

So, we can book you for some more sessions. We will have to have a few sessions till your body is fully restored.

**JODHI**

That will be fine.

**HUA**

It was very good to meet you, Mr Livingstone. I like what you believe.

**JODHI**

Thanks. It was great meeting you. Next time you can maybe join us for a BBQ with Emma and Ernst at our place.

**HUA**

That would be lovely.

**JODHI**

Have a great day. You've got it, Hua, you've got it. (*Jodhi is laughing.*)

**HUA**

True, I look forward to seeing you again, Mr Livingstone.

***Next Scene***

*(Scene of Jodhi, Helen, Christian, Jessica, Ernst, Emma, and their daughter Mulan together with Ann and Hua and her husband at Jodhi's house.)*

*(Christian and Jessica are in the swimming pool playing with Mulan while the others are sitting at a table at the pool. The fire is on for the BBQ. The song plays **"Summertime Chi" by Lee Foss, John Summit, and Hayley May.)***

**JODHI**

So, Hua, we are delighted to have you and your husband here with us.

**HUA**

We are more than happy to be here.

**EMMA**

Jodhi, you have a lot of Chinese friends now. We are actually half of the guest list. (*Emma is smiling.)*

**JODHI**

China represents such a large population on earth. I should have even more Chinese friends. (*Jodhi is smiling.)*

**EMMA**

The children seem to enjoy themselves playing in the pool. I am happy your children are looking after little Mulan.

**JODHI**

Well, both Christian and Jessica had swimming lessons from an early age, so Mulan is in very safe hands.

**EMMA**

That's great. So, Ann is helping Jodhi and Helen in the bank they have set up together.

**HUA**

Wow. Is that the 888 Bank?

**JODHI**

Yes, that's correct. We have set it up for our time so that we have an alternative when the United Nations make it legally compulsory to have a chip on your hand or forehead, the mark of the beast.

**HUA**

Well, I will definitely be joining your bank.

**JODHI**

It's going to be important for all of God's people. We are clearly warned in the Book of Revelation not to take the chip on the forehand or on the forehead.

**HUA**

What will happen with the people that do take the chip?

**JODHI**

It's a matter of no return. Once you have it, then it's all over.

**HUA**

Wow, that's very serious.

**JODHI**

Yes, it is. They have full control of your decisions. You become half human and half robot.

**HUA**

Ann, where did you meet Jodhi and Helen?

**ANN**

I met them in Rome. It was one of those divine encounters.

**JODHI**

Yes, ironically, it was in Rome when the Pope announced to the world that we should follow the New World Order.

**HUA**

So, what does the 888 stands for in the bank you have created?

**JODHI**

Well, I know 8 is a lucky number in China. In Christian numerology, the number 888 represents Jesus or, more specifically, Christ the Redeemer.
The representation may be justified either through gematria, by counting the letter values of the Greek transliteration of Jesus's name, or as an opposing value to 666, the number of the Beast.

**ANN**

If I am correct, the people that are marked by God are opposed to the people that are marked by the Beast?

**JODHI**

That's correct. That's why the 2 witnesses are in Rome now. To warn people against taking the Mark of the Beast.

***Scene goes back to Rome***

*(Boaz and Jachin are with their wives having a coffee in the same coffee shop where Jodhi, Helen and Ann went to Rome. They discuss the next steps to follow.)*

**BOAZ**

Well, guys, I think our work here is done for now.

**JACHIN**

Agreed.

**BOAZ**

I think the next step is for Rachel and me to go back to Los Angeles to fulfil our next mission.

**JACHIN**

Yeah, I also think Suyin and me should go to Hong Kong for our important mission there.

**BOAZ**

Before we leave Rome, I feel the Lord has spoken to me about buying a sackcloth robe.

**JACHIN**

Yeah, I understand what you mean brother. The Lord spoke with me also about it.

**SUCHIN**

Is that part of the mission?

**BOAZ**

Yes, very much so. It is making a statement that God is serious about this time!

**RACHEL**

Well, when Suyin and I went shopping earlier, I saw this tailor-made clothing company. They make any clothing to your specific request.

**BOAZ**

Well, that sounds like the right place. Unfortunately, we can't get Armani suits, but at least they can make some high-end sackcloth robes. (*Everyone is laughing.)*

*Next Scene*

*(The 4 of them enter the Clothing shop and speak to the manageress Claudia.)*

**BOAZ**

Good day Madam.

**MANAGERESS CLAUDIA**

Good day Sir. How can I help you?

**BOAZ**

We were wondering if you could design some robes for us?

**MANAGERESS CLAUDIA**

Sure Sir. What did you have in mind?

**BOAZ**

We are looking for 2 robes in sackcloth.

**MANAGERESS CLAUDIA**

Well, that is a first for us. Which colour are you looking at?

**BOAZ**

I will go for light blue.

**JACHIN**

I will go for black.

**BOAZ**

I knew that. You are the man in black. (*Boaz is laughing.)*

***(The song play "Man in Black" by Johnny Cash.)***

**MANAGERESS CLAUDIA**

Ok, we will take your measurements and get it made for you.

**BOAZ**

How long will it take?

**MANAGERESS CLAUDIA**

3 days.

**BOAZ**

Thanks, we will be back in 3 days' time.

*(They leave the shop. Claudia is talking to her assistant and tells her that she recognised Boaz and Jachin from the TV when they were preaching in front of St. Peter Basilica.)*

**MANAGERESS CLAUDIA**

Do you know who was in our shop right now?

**ASSISTANT SOPHIA**

I have seen them somewhere.

**MANAGERESS CLAUDIA**

They are the preachers that preached in front of the St. Peter Basilica. I saw them on TV. It was all over the news.

**ASSISTANT SOPHIA**

*Si.* (Subtitles: yes)

*(They both are in awe.)*

*Next Scene*

*(Boaz, Rachel, Jachin and Suyin are at the airport saying goodbye to each other. Boaz and Jachin both have their robes on.)*

**BOAZ**

Well, guys, the real work starts now.

**JACHIN**

Yip. God be with us.

**RACHEL**

God is with all of us, so nothing to fear.

**SUCHIN**

God bless you.

*(They all hug each other. They go to board 2 different planes.)*

*Next Scene*

*(Boaz and Rachel arrived at LA. They are sitting outside a restaurant overlooking Hollywood Mountain. They are having a coffee.)*

**BOAZ**

It's nice to be back.

**RACHEL**

Yes, it is.

**BOAZ**

The only thing is whether they are going to like us after this.

**RACHEL**

Well, Boaz, not everyone needs to like you, only me. (*Rachel is smiling.)*

**BOAZ**

That's for sure. It is going to be true in a minute. (*Boaz is smiling.)*

**RACHEL**

What do you mean?

**BOAZ**

You remember Jesus's first miracle. (*Boaz is winking at Rachel.)*

**RACHEL**

You are not going to do that, right?

**BOAZ**

Do you see that lady in red sitting with her boyfriend at the table to the right?

*(She is drinking a glass of water.)*

**RACHEL**

Oh, my word, you are going to do it.

**BOAZ**

Look. (*Boaz is pointing with his eyes in her direction.)*

*(The lady's water turns into blood. She is screaming. The whole restaurant is looking at the scene in awe. Boaz and Rachel are standing up and paying their bill. Boaz is saying to the people something before he leaves.)*

**BOAZ**

I guess the end has begun. (*Boaz is walking off with Rachel.)*

***Next Scene***

*(A scene at the Venetian Casino in Macau, China, with Jachin and Suyin.)*

*(They are entering the Casino.)*

**JACHIN**

Well, Suyin, have you ever been to a Casino before?

**SUYIN**

Never.

**JACHIN**

Me neither. *(Jachin is smiling.)*

**SUYIN**

What are we going to do here?

**JACHIN**

Wait and see. We are going to have some fun.

*(They are walking towards the middle of the Casino. To the right is the billionaire Mr Chan playing Black Jack again. They stop in the middle of the Casino. Looking at everything around them.)*

**JACHIN**

Wow, is this what a Casino looks like?

**SUYIN**

It's massive.

**JACHIN**

Yeah, apparently, it's the second-biggest casino in the world.

**SUYIN**

Really?

**JACHIN**

Yes, I am glad we chose this one.

**SUYIN**

Why?

**JACHIN**

Because the bigger the venue, the bigger the impact.

**SUYIN**

What do you mean?

**JACHIN**

Well, we are going to write Jesus's name all over this Casino.

**SUYIN**

How exactly are we going to do that?

**JACHIN**

Watch carefully. Do you see all the numbers on the machines?

**SUYIN**

There are so many machines.

**JACHIN**

Indeed.

*(Jachin is turning all the numbers to 888. The people start realising what is going on. They call for assistance. People are losing money everywhere in the Casino. There are loud voices. Management and security are coming to intervene.)*

*(Jachin and Suyin are leaving the casino. Before they leave, Jachin is speaking in a loud voice to the people.)*

**JACHIN**

It looks like God is in the building.

**THE SECURITY GUARD**

*(Talking to Jachin.)*

Hey, man in black. Where are you going?

**JACHIN**

To a better place than this. *(Jachin and Suyin are leaving the building.)*

***Next Scene in LA***

*(Boaz and Rachel have left the restaurant. They are walking on Sunset Boulevard.)*

**RACHEL**

Where are we going, Boaz?

**BOAZ**

To our next mission.

**RACHEL**

Do you mean that was not enough for today?

**BOAZ**

No, it's never-ending until the end. We have just started.

**RACHEL**

You must be kidding.

**BOAZ**

Yeah, I want everyone in town to know us by the end of the day. *(Boaz is laughing.)*

**RACHEL**

What are we going to do next?

**BOAZ**

I am going to get a taxi for us to Mount Lee.

*(Boaz is stopping a taxi. The taxi driver's name is Edward. He is taking them to Mount Lee.)*

**TAXI DRIVER EDWARD**

So, you guys are going to see Mount Lee.

**BOAZ**

Yeah, man. We are going to light it up, big time!

**TAXI DRIVER EDWARD**

Do you mean like a fire show?

**BOAZ**

Something like that.

**TAXI DRIVER EDWARD**

That would be great. I haven't seen a fire show up there yet.

**BOAZ**

There is always a first time. We will make sure it's special.

**TAXI DRIVER EDWARD**

Like special effects?

**BOAZ**

Yeah, something like that. (*Boaz is smiling.)*

**TAXI DRIVER EDWARD**

I don't see any fire rockets with you.

**BOAZ**

Don't worry, cowboy, it's going to be fine. I have what I need.

*(The taxi driver is dropping them off.)*

**TAXI DRIVER EDWARD**

Good luck, guys. Enjoy your fire show.

**BOAZ**

Thanks.

*(Boaz and Rachel go up the mountain at the road close to the Hollywood sign on the mountain.)*

**BOAZ**

You know what, Rachel?

**RACHEL**

No Boaz. You always have me baffled. I don't know what's next. You are the great Puzzler. *(Rachel is smiling.)*

**BOAZ**

You see that sign.

**RACHEL**

Yes, Boaz, we have seen that sign many times. It's not like we are not from LA.

**BOAZ**

Well, that sign is going to change.

**RACHEL**

Really Boaz. How are you going to do it this time? *(Rachel is smiling.)*

**BOAZ**

I am going to change it to the original meaning.

**RACHEL**

I bet you are.

**BOAZ**

Yeah, but not yet.

**RACHEL**

What are you going to do first?

**BOAZ**

We are going to enjoy some blazing fireworks first.

**RACHEL**

Right, I love fireworks.

**BOAZ**

Ok, good. Ready?

**RACHEL**

Always Boaz.

**BOAZ**

Here we go.

*(Boaz is commanding fire and lightning to strike down on the mountain. Everything is on fire. The fire service is coming out. Before they reach the mountain, Boaz stops the fire. The sign has changed to "The City of Angels".)*

**RACHEL**

This is going to be funny. It looks like 10's of fire trucks are arriving. There is no fire. What are they going to do? (*Rachel is smiling.)*

**BOAZ**

Wait till they see the signpost change to "City of Angels."

*(The fire service stops at the place where Boaz and Rachel are standing. They start talking with Boaz and Rachel. The Media is also arriving.)*

**FIRE BRIGADE CAPTAIN**

Hey, you guys. What is happening here? We all saw the fire and lighting coming to the mountain. We don't get it. Where is it now?

**BOAZ**

I guess God put it out.

**FIRE BRIGADE CAPTAIN**

Don't joke. This was an enormous big fire, an inferno of epic proportions.

**BOAZ**

Well, God is big and bright, right?

**FIRE BRIGADE CAPTAIN**

You are a joker.

**BOAZ**

No, Sir, I don't play card games. No jokers in this pack.

**FIRE BRIGADE CAPTAIN**

My word, no point trying to speak to you!

**FIRE BRIGADE ASSISTANT**

Captain, look at the sign board. This is crazy.
*(They all look at the signpost on the mountain.)*

**FIRE BRIGADE CAPTAIN**

My God! Who changed the signpost?!!! City of Angels???

**BOAZ**

Sir, I told you. This was the work of God.

**FIRE BRIGADE CAPTAIN**

Can you please shut up?!

**BOAZ**

No Sir. You have to change the constitutional laws for that, remember "Freedom of Speech"?

*(The media arrives. They are taking shots of what is happening. Boaz is talking to a media guy, and then he and Rachel are off.)*

**MEDIA GUY**

How did you end up here?

**BOAZ**

We wanted to go to the mountain. Then all the action happened.

**MEDIA GUY**

What did you see?

**BOAZ**

We saw God light up the whole mountain.

**MEDIA GUY**

For real?

**BOAZ**

Yes. Then the fire spread everywhere, and it stopped after 30 min.

**MEDIA GUY**

Wow, and then?

**BOAZ**

We saw the signboard saying "City of Angels".

**MEDIA GUY**

You are right. It says "City of Angels".

**BOAZ**

We have to go now. It was nice meeting you.

**MEDIA GUY**

Same to you.

*(Boaz and Rachel are going off the mountain. They call upon a Saints 888 taxi to take them home.)*

***Next Scene***

*(They are back home. They are talking about the day.)*

**BOAZ**

That was great today. What do you think?

**RACHEL**

A bit out of the normal, but, hey, let's see. We definitely will be in the news. (*Rachel is smiling.)*

**BOAZ**

Let's see what is on Fox News.

*(Rachel is putting the TV on Fox News. LA Scene on Lee mountain comes up. They are on the news having a chat with the Media guy.)*

**RACHEL**

I told you we would be on the news.

**BOAZ**

Yeah, no worries, that's the way it has to be.

*(The song plays* ***"It's Time for the reign of God" by Brian Doerksen****.)*

**BOAZ**

It's time. I need to phone Jachin.

*(Boaz is phoning Jachin. Jachin picks up.)*

**JACHIN**

Hello brother Boaz! What's up?

**BOAZ**

Well, we put Hollywood mountain on fire, but it's all cool.

**JACHIN**

Well done. We had fun in the Casino too. I don't think anyone is going there soon. *( Jachin is smiling.)*

**BOAZ**

Good man. Jachin, the reason for the call is I think the Lord is speaking to me about stopping the rain. What do you sense?

**JACHIN**

Amen. I agree. I had a dream last night that all the clouds couldn't give any rain anymore.

**BOAZ**

Well, that is it, then. We are going to be very unpopular, but hey, we serve the One and Only. Let's do it. His command is our privilege to obey.

**JACHIN**

I suggest we pray tonight and ask the Lord because His timing is always perfect.

**BOAZ**

I agree, brother.

### *Next Scene*

*(It is in the evening both Boaz and Jachin pray to the Lord. Jesus appears to Boaz.)*

**JESUS**

Boaz, I heard you and Jachin's prayers. Indeed, this is the time that I want you to stop the rain. This is part of the sign that your mission has begun. The world has 42 months left before My return. In these 42 months, I will shake the nations like never before, and they will get to know that I am the real meaning of Life. This is part of My Grace period so that people will turn to Me before My great return. Tomorrow morning at 9 am LA Time, go to Santa Monica beach and command the rain to stop. I will speak with Jachin to do the same. My word must be fulfilled. When 2 people agree in My name, it shall be done. Amen.

*(Jesus disappears.)*

***New Scene***

*(It's 9am in LA. It's raining. Boaz is at Santa Monica Beach. He is at the signpost of trail 66. Then he walks unto the beach towards the sea. Before he reaches the water, he stops. He starts praying for the rain to stop worldwide.)*

*Next Scene*

*(Jesus appears to Jachin.)*

**JESUS**

Jachin, it's time for you and Boaz to start your Ministry. You are like John the Baptist to prepare the way for Me. I have chosen you for this important time before My return. Go to Big Wave Beach and command the rain to stop. The Big Wave is symbolic of My Great Power that I am going to release in this hour. Be brave and trust Me.

*(Jesus disappears.)*

*(In another scene, Jachin is at Big Wave Beach, Hong Kong, also praying on the beach for the rain to stop.*

*Different scenes follow of places in the world where the rain suddenly stops.)*

*Next Scene*

*(Ernst is watching on TV the news events at his home in Blouberg, Cape Town. Emma is sitting next to him and Mulan. They see news reports. People are confused. There is no rain anywhere in the world. Ernst is talking with Emma.)*

**ERNST**

See Emma, people only become serious when God becomes serious.

**EMMA**

Yeah, it's going to be an interesting time to watch how things unfold everywhere in the world.

**ERNST**

For sure.

**EMMA**

I think we will see a very rapid increase in flight bookings on our airline from now on.

**ERNST**

Yeah, they will start recognising that Southern Africa is indeed the place of safety in the coming days, the end of days.

**EMMA**

What is that scripture again? I think Isaiah 54:10 is the one... My covenant of peace will not be shaken.

**ERNST**

That's correct. While the world is shaken, God's covenant of peace remains with His people.

*Next Scene*

*(Scene where Jodhi and Helen are walking on Blouberg Beach. They are holding hands. They are talking about their wedding at the Blue Peter Hotel at Blouberg Beach.)*

**JODHI**

Remember our wedding was here. It was out of this world.

**HELEN**

Yeah, how could I forget? It was the best day of my life.

*(Jodhi is giving Helen a kiss.)*

**JODHI**

We have made a lot of new friends since then.

**HELEN**

Yeah, it was great meeting Boaz and Jachin with their wives.

**JODHI**

Indeed, I wonder how they are doing?

**HELEN**

We must contact them again, but I think they are very busy with their mission.

**JODHI**

I am sure they are.

*Next Scene*

*(Boaz is in his bed awakened by a visitation of Jesus. Rachel is still sleeping. Jesus is speaking to Boaz.)*

**JESUS**

Boaz, it is time to mark My people as they are about to bring out the law for people to take the Mark of the Beast. I will speak to Jachin as one of My angels is starting first from the East to mark My Saints. Be strong as you will need to face a lot of battles in the days to come.

*(Jesus disappears.)*

***Next Scene***

*(Jachin is in his garden tending to the Lilies. He receives an open vision from the Lord.)*

**JESUS**

Jachin, hear me. As you are giving water to these Lilies, I have come as the Lily of the Valley so that My bride can be marked by My name. I have 4 angels standing at the 4 corners of the earth to prevent any wind from blowing on the land or the sea or any tree. I am sending another angel coming from the East that has the seal of the living God. He is about to come.

*(Jesus disappears.)*

*Next Scene*

*(The Angel with the seal of God arrives from the East, standing in the clouds above Tokyo.*

*He is calling out in a loud voice to the four angels who had been given the power to harm the land and the sea.)*

**ANGEL WITH THE SEAL OF GOD**

**ALL VISUAL**

"Do not harm the land and the sea or the trees until we put a seal on the foreheads of the servants of our God."

*(Thousands of Angels gather together around the Archangel. They are going through the earth from the East to the West and mark the Saints that have been ready for the hour.*

***Next Scene***

*In a scene where Jachin is at the great wall of China in Beijing. He is proclaiming the word of God. 42 people gather on the bridge mocking him. A Panda bear is coming out on the bridge, and karate kicks all of them off the bridge.*

***Next Scene***

*A scene, Boaz is on King Ranch near Kingsville, Texas. He commands a plague on all the cattle on the ranch to die. There are large screams coming from everywhere as people start to realise what's happening. The neighbouring farms in Texas are hit by the same plague as Boaz extends it to the rest of the farms.)*

***Next Scene***

*(A scene follows where Ernst and Emma are at Jodhi and Helen's home. Emma is organising the release of more planes from her phone to different airports so that people can fly to Southern Africa. Jodhi is reading from the bible to his daughter, Jessica. She is asking him questions about it.)*

**JODHI**

*(Jodhi is reading Amos 9:11)*

"On that day, I will raise up
The tabernacle of David, which has fallen down,
And repair its damages;
I will raise up its ruins,
And rebuild it as in the days of old."

**JESSICA**

What is a tabernacle?

**JODHI**

It means dwelling place or residence. As for you, our house is your residence.

**JESSICA**

So, why do they call it the tabernacle of David?

**JODHI**

Good question, Jessica. It means the House of David. Your name Jessica comes from the name Jesse who was the father of King David.

**JESSICA**

So, I am the only one in the House of David in our family?

**JODHI**

*(Jodhi is laughing.)* We all are because the House of David is a metaphor for the House of God.

**JESSICA**

So, why is it about rebuilding the House of God?

**JODHI**

It's like bringing all the family of God together in one dwelling place. In this case, it's the fulfilment of the prophecy.

*Next Scene*

*(Willem Van Der Merwe is on outreach in Soweto, South Africa. He is telling the people not to take the Mark of the Beast but to trust God. His team are handing out leaflets of Saints 888 Bank. Ann is in charge of the distribution of the leaflets. Wikus speaks over a microphone to a crowd who gathers there.)*

**WILLEM VAN DER MERWE**

People of Soweto. Be aware today not to take the Mark of The Beast that the New World Order is introducing to you. Let me read you the scripture that warns us against it and tells the outcome of it.

Speaking of the Beast. In Revelation 13:16-17, we read. "He causes all, both small and great, rich and poor, free and slave, to receive a mark on their right hand or on their foreheads, [17] and that no one may buy or sell except one who has the mark or the name of the beast, or the number of his name. Here is wisdom. Let him who has understanding calculate the number of the beast, for it is the number of a man: His number *is* 666.

If a person takes the mark of the Beast, there is no turning back. Let's see what Revelations 16:1-2 says. "Then I heard a loud voice from the temple saying to the seven angels, "Go and pour out the bowls of the wrath of God on the earth." [2] So the first went and poured out his bowl upon the earth, and a foul and loathsome sore came upon the men who had the mark of the beast and those who worshipped his image."

*(A guy in the crowd is speaking to his friend.)*

**THE GUY IN THE CROWD**

Is this not the brother of that guy that played in the movie District 9?

**HIS FRIEND**

My chommy (Subtitles: friend), you are right, that is his brother.

**THE GUY IN THE CROWD**

I think we should listen to him. Look, his brother turned into a prawn robot in that movie. He is warning all of us not to take the mark of the beast; otherwise, we can turn into prawn robots too!

**HIS FRIEND**

Yes, I have a family, and I don't want that to happen to me.

*(Willem is giving the microphone to Ann. She is speaking with the people about God's bank and an alternative system to buy and sell.)*

***Next Scene***

*(Jodhi, Christian and Ann are meeting Solomon regarding gold business at the Sun International hotel in Sandton. They are sitting at the outside area. While waiting for Solomon, Jodhi is speaking to Christian about Haggai 2:6-8)*

**JODHI**

You see, Christian. All the gold and silver belong to God. See what God is saying in Haggai 2:6-8

*(Jodhi is reading from his iPad.)*

" For thus says the Lord of hosts: 'Once more (it *is* a little while) I will shake heaven and earth, the sea and dry land; [7] and I will shake all nations, and they shall come to the Desire of All Nations, and I will fill this temple with glory,' says the Lord of hosts. [8] 'The silver *is* Mine, and the gold *is* Mine,' says the Lord of hosts."

**CHRISTIAN**

Is that part specifically speaking about today?

**JODHI**

Yes, it was relevant at that time when the foundation stone was laid of the Second temple in Jerusalem, but it refers very much to today also.

**CHRISTIAN**

That's excellent.

*(Solomon arrives. He greets everyone. Jodhi starts a conversation with him.)*

**JODHI**

So good to see you again, Solomon.

**SOLOMON**

Good to see you guys. I am also happy to be in South Africa.

**JODHI**

So, Solomon, this is my son Christian, and this is Ann.

**SOLOMON**

Nice to meet you guys.

**JODHI**

Christian is my righthand man in the business. He will handle the contract we make with you while Ann is managing the online bank for us. So, I hope you have brought us some good deals from the mines.

**SOLOMON**

Yeah, for sure. We have some offers on the table from Congo, Kenya and Tanzania.

**JODHI**

That's good news. Let's see what you have, as our time is short. We have to catch a flight to Cape Town for a meeting in Cape Town with De Beers for diamonds.

**SOLOMON**

No problem.

*(They are signing the contracts and are saying goodbye.)*

***Next Scene***

*(Jodhi, Christian and Ann are meeting with a couple from De Beers Diamonds in the Waterfront, Cape Town. They are signing a contract too.)*

**JODHI**

It's a pleasure doing business with you, Mark. Glad De Beers is still in good hands, and not everyone in it is sold out to this world.

**MARK**

Me and Jen are always glad to help the good guys in this world, Mr Livingstone.

**JODHI**

That's good to hear. God will reward you for that.

**MARK**

Thank you.

**JODHI**

Well, it's time to go. Our team here has done enough business for one day.

*(They are all shaking hands and saying goodbye to each other.)*

***Next Scene***

*(Scene with Boaz in Miami. He is releasing locusts from Miami beach to the city. The city is full of locusts. People are running indoors for shelter. Rachel is with Boaz.)*

**RACHEL**

Why locusts at this time, Boaz?

**BOAZ**

Because the locusts are like an army that brings destruction to the world. God is raising up an army in Southern Africa to do great work. It's a reminder to His saints to relocate to a place where God wants His army to come together on parade. Like in the book of Joel in the Bible.

**RACHEL**

It looks like every plague has a meaning, just like the 10 plagues of Moses.

**BOAZ**

Yeah, my sweet Rachel, you are like the wife of Moses, Zipporah, in the Bible.

**RACHEL**

I see that. Like the saying says, "behind every strong man is a strong woman."

**BOAZ**

Exactly. (*Boaz is kissing Rachel.)* Well, that's true too. They both are smiling at each other.

*Next Scene*

*(Jachin is with Suyin at a Buddha Temple in Bangkok, Thailand.)*

**JACHIN**

Suyin, you know what?

**SUYIN**

Tell me.

**JACHIN**

Old temples whose foundations are not built on Christ will fall.

*(Suddenly, the whole temple falls to pieces. You see cracks appearing everywhere in the walls and people running out of the temple. A statue of Buddha falls to the ground.)*

**JACHIN**

I don't think people will soon return to this temple.

**SUYIN**

There is no temple to return to. It's all in ruins.

**JACHIN**

Do you know what's next, Suyin?

**SUCHIN**

Tell me Jachin.

**JACHIN**

Have you ever experienced teleporting?

**SUYIN**

Never, neither did you. I know you that well. (*Suyin is smiling at Jachin.)*

**JACHIN**

That's right, but there is always a first time for us. (*Jachin is smiling.)*

**SUYIN**

Where are we going?

**JACHIN**

You will see.

*Next Scene*

*(Jachin and Suyin appear at the foot of Mount Everest.)*

**SUYIN**

Wow. Gosh, I never thought in my whole life this would happen to me! And, what is this enormous mountain that is in front of us? It looks like Mount Everest.

**JACHIN**

It is Mount Everest?! *(Jachin is laughing.)*

**SUYIN**

But it does not even feel cold here.

**JACHIN**

It's because of the supernatural warmth of God's presence around us.

**SUYIN**

This is all beyond me. What are we going to do here?

**JACHIN**

We are going to show the world that the blood of Christ has redeemed us from all sin, and salvation belongs to Him.

**SUYIN**

How are you going to do that exactly?

**JACHIN**

Well, let me show you.
*(Jachin reaches out his hand to the mountain and commands that the ice turns into blood. Suddenly, the whole mountain is covered in blood.)*

**SUYIN**

I have no words.

**JACHIN**

Neither have I; I am only an instrument in God's hand.

(*They stand in awe, watching the view on the mountain.)*

***Next Scene***

*( A Scene of Boaz and Rachel that are in Dubai in Business Bay overlooking the Burj Khalifa.)*

**BOAZ**

You know Rachel, why God doesn't like these tall buildings?

**RACHEL**

Why?

**BOAZ**

It is because of what they represent.

**RACHEL**

What does it represent?

**BOAZ**

Pride. Do you know what God says about pride?

**RACHEL**

Pride comes before a fall. It's called hubris.

**BOAZ**

Boom, you got it. That's why this building is coming down.

*(While Boaz is talking, a lightning rod whizzes from the sky and hits the top of the tower. Then the whole building gets struck by lightning. It starts collapsing. People are running everywhere)*

**RACHEL**

Wow, is that what happened to the Tower of Babel?

**BOAZ**

Yeah, I guess something like that.

***Next Scene***

*(Jodhi and Helen are sitting in their garden. They are holding hands.)*

**HELEN**

Do you remember the first time when we were flying together to New York?

**JODHI**

How could I forget it? It feels like yesterday.

**HELEN**

Yes, it sure does. It was so exciting. Our first trip together.

**JODHI**

Well, it worked out well. Don't you think?

**HELEN**

I wouldn't change anything for being with you. (*They are kissing.)*

**JODHI**

We still have some things ahead of us before this world comes to an end.

**HELEN**

Very true, but even after this life, we are forever together for Eternity.

**JODHI**

You couldn't have said it better. (*They give each other a big hug.*)

*(Christian and Jessica are outside in the garden playing ball.)*

***Next Scene***

*(Ernst and Emma are watching the news events unfolding on TV. The war in Jerusalem is on full-scale.)*

**ERNST**

Wow, another prophecy has come into fulfilment.

**EMMA**

Which one is that?

**ERNST**

I will read it to you.

*(Ernst goes on google on his phone and looks up Luke 21:20-24.)*

[20] "But when you see Jerusalem surrounded by armies, then know that its desolation is near. [21] Then let those who are in Judea flee to the mountains, let those who are in the midst of her depart, and let not those who are in the country enter her.[22] For these are the days of vengeance that all things which are written may be fulfilled. [23] But woe to those who are pregnant and to those who are nursing babies in those days! For there will be great distress in the land and wrath upon this people. [24] And they will fall by the edge of the sword and be led away captive into all nations. And Jerusalem will be trampled by Gentiles until the times of the Gentiles are fulfilled."

**EMMA**

So, when are the times of the Gentiles completed?

**ERNST**

You have to understand Daniel's 70-year prophecy.

**EMMA**

Could you please explain that?

**ERNST**

Sure honey. (*Ernst gives Emma a kiss.)*

It's all in the Book of Daniel, Chapter 9.

Let me read it to you.

Verse 24-27

24"Seventy weeks are determined
For your people and for your holy city,
To finish the transgression,
To make an end of sins,
To make reconciliation for iniquity,
To bring in everlasting righteousness,
To seal up vision and prophecy,
And to anoint the Most Holy.

25 "Know therefore and understand,
That from the going forth of the command
To restore and build Jerusalem
Until Messiah the Prince,
There shall be seven weeks and sixty-two weeks;
The street shall be built again, and the wall,
Even in troublesome times.

26 And after the sixty-two weeks
Messiah shall be cut off, but not for Himself;
And the people of the prince who is to come
Shall destroy the city and the sanctuary.
The end of it shall be with a flood,
And till the end of the war desolations are determined.
27 Then he shall confirm a covenant with many for one week;
But in the middle of the week
He shall bring an end to sacrifice and offering.
And on the wing of abominations shall be one who makes desolate,
Even until the consummation, which is determined,
Is poured out on the desolate."

**EMMA**

So, what are the 70 weeks about?

**ERNST**

It is 176,400 days. (*Ernst is smiling.)*

**EMMA**

What?? How in this world have you come to that number?

**ERNST**

The 70 weeks are 70 multiplied by 7 days which are 490 days.

**EMMA**

I thought it was 176,400 days.

**ERNST**

It is. Each day stands for a year. In the time of Daniel, a year was 360 days.

**EMMA**

So why is it made so difficult to understand?

**ERNST**

It's like a treasure, a puzzle; you have to seek it out, almost like you. (*Ernst is winking at Emma.)*

**EMMA**

*(Emma is smiling.)* When did the 70 years weeks started?

**ERNST**

It started with the decree from the Persian king Artaxerxes to rebuild the city, which dates to the 14th of March 445 BC.

**EMMA**

Does Messiah the Prince refer to Jesus?

**ERNST**

Correct.

**EMMA**

So, after 7 weeks and 62 weeks, the Messiah the Prince came on the scene?

**ERNST**

Correct again. You are not just a pretty face but smart too.

**EMMA**

I think you married me more for my looks than me trying to be smarter than you.
*(Emma is smiling at Ernst.)*

**ERNST**

I think for both. (*Ernst gives Emma a kiss.)*

**EMMA**

So, tell me more about the 7 weeks and the 62 weeks.

**ERNST**

Well, from the 14$^{th}$ of March, 445 BC, to the 6th of April, 32AD, it is exactly 69 weeks. So, from the time of the decree to Jesus's triumphant entry into Jerusalem with a donkey, the 69 weeks were completed.

**EMMA**

You know your stuff. Was that on Palm Sunday, which we celebrate till today?

**ERNST**

Yes. His followers recognised the significance of the day and received Him with praise: "Blessed is the King who comes in the name of the Lord!"

**EMMA**

So, the part where it says the Messiah will be cut off must refer to His crucifixion?

**ERNST**

Yeah.

**EMMA**

So, what about the final week?

**ERNST**

There is a big gap of 2000 years between the end of the 69$^{th}$ week and the beginning of the 70$^{th}$ week.

**EMMA**

So, the 70$^{th}$ week has already started?

**ERNST**

Yes, it started when the peace treaty was signed in 2033 with Israel. We are now at the part where Syria broke that peace treaty and attacked Israel.

**EMMA**

Ok. Now I fully understand; that's why we are in the last 42 months before Christ returns to earth.

**ERNST**

You got it in one, number one.

**EMMA**

Everything is starting to make sense.

**ERNST**

Yeah, that's why Boaz and Jachin are out there fulfilling their 42 months of ministry.

**EMMA**

It's so amazing that we have met all these people. It feels like we are part of an Avenger movie.

**ERNST**

Yeah. Who knows, maybe we are the real Avengers! (*They both are smiling at each other.)*

***Next Scene***

*(It's Valentine's day. Jachin is with Suyin in Singapore. They drive past Raffles hotel on their way to a wedding dress shop. Suyin is confused as to why they are going to a wedding dress shop. They arrive at the wedding dress shop. He is talking to Suyin.)*

**JACHIN**

Happy Valentine's day, my love.

**SUYIN**

You too, honey. (*They kiss each other.)*

**JACHIN**

Suyin, I feel like doing something beautiful today instead of upsetting people.

**SUYIN**

That would be good for a change, but I still don't know why we are here. (*Suyin is looking confused.)*

**JACHIN**

Let's see what this shop locks like inside.

*(They are going into the shop. A shop assistant asks if she could help them.)*

**SHOP ASSISTANT**

Morning.

**JACHIN**

Good morning.

**SHOP ASSISTANT**

Could I assist you with anything?

**JACHIN**

We are just here to see how your wedding dresses look.

**SHOP ASSISTANT**

That's great. I take it you are in love. You want to get married?

**SUYIN**

We are already married. You must ask my husband. I don't know why we are here.
*(The shop assistant is looking at Jachin.)*

**JACHIN**

I am looking for many wedding dresses as a lot of people I know are getting married soon.

*(Suyin is looking in amazement at Jachin.)*

**SHOP ASSISTANT**

That's good news. I am sure my manageress will be well pleased with that.

**JACHIN**

I am sure she will be.

*(Jachin is looking at the dresses in the shop.)*

Well, it all looks good. Thanks for your time. I just want a quick word with my wife outside.

**SHOP ASSISTANT**

No problem. Come back anytime.

*(Jachin and Suyin leave the shop.)*

**SUYIN**

Are you going bananas?

**JACHIN**

You haven't seen yet what I am going to do. (*Jachin is smiling.)*

*(Jachin changes the name of Singapore Brides shop to 'The Bride of Christ'. The wedding dresses turn into glittering white wedding dresses, all with the name tag 'Bride of Christ'.)*

***Next Scene***

*Boaz is walking with Rachel in front of Candy Bar, nearing Tigerlily Boutique hotel in Edinburgh.*

**BOAZ**

You know what, Rachel?

**RACHEL**

Tell me, Boaz.

**BOAZ**

I am still in love with you. The day I lay my eyes on you was the greatest day of my life!

***('You're still the one' by Shania Twain plays.)***

**RACHEL**

Awh. You are still my superhero. (*They kiss each other.)*

**BOAZ**

Jachin texted me about something beautiful that he did yesterday on Valentine's Day in Singapore. As it's Valentine's day today here, I thought I should do something beautiful too.

*(They are in front of Tigerlily Boutique hotel. On Boaz's command, the whole front lights up with a big red heart with Jesus's name in the middle. The people outside witness this. They are mesmerised.)*

### *Next Scene*

*(Jodhi and Helen are celebrating Valentine's day at the Blue Peter Hotel in Cape Town, where they got married. The whole hotel belongs to Christians. They are using Saints 888 Bank for all transactions.)*

**JODHI**

It feels so nice to be back, Helen.

**HELEN**

Yes. It's such a pleasant surprise that you booked a table here at our wedding venue. This is our special place.

**JODHI**

Well, I thought this would be the perfect venue for us on Valentine's Day.

*(They give each other a kiss. )*

**HELEN**

Jodhi, I am so glad I married you.

**JODHI**

Why Mrs beautiful?

**HELEN**

Because you are my hero and such a romantic.

**JODHI**

Thank you, but wait till I tell you this story.

**HELEN**

Another one of your many stories. (*Helen is smiling.)* I can't wait. Tell me. (*Helen is winking at Jodhi.)*

**JODHI**

Well, you remember the story of Jacob in the Bible when he fled from his brother to go to another country.

**HELEN**

Of course. Then he met his Rachel. Love at first sight, remember? *(Helen is smiling.)*

**JODHI**

Yeah. (*Jodhi is smiling at Helen.*) You are my Rachel. From the very first day, I saw you, I fell in love with you. (*Jodhi is kissing Helen.)*

**HELEN**

You can always kiss me. I don't mind. (*Helen is smiling at Jodhi.)*

**JODHI**

Indeed, I will. I can't stop kissing you. (*Jodhi kisses Helen again.)*

**HELEN**

Remind me again. Why again did Jacob flee from his brother?

**JODHI**

He fled because he took his brother's inheritance and birthright.
So, while he was on his journey to his relatives, he used a stone as a pillow when he slept in the field. He had a dream that angels were going up and down from heaven to earth.

**HELEN**

Yeah, I know that story well. He called the stone the House of God.

**JODHI**

Yeah, it's called the Stone of Destiny or the Bethel stone. It's been kept at Edinburgh Castle since 1996.

**HELEN**

I heard that all the British Kings and Queens were anointed on it.

**JODHI**

That's true, but also, all the kings of Israel were anointed on it until Jeremiah the prophet brought it to Ireland. That's how it landed up in Britain.

**HELEN**

Interesting story. (*Helen gives Jodhi a hug.)*

***Next Scene***

*( Ernst is speaking with Emma about organising a BBQ with Atif and his family.)*

**ERNST**

Good morning, lovely. (*Ernst gives Emma a kiss.)*

**EMMA**

Good morning honey. Here is your coffee.

**ERNST**

Thanks a million. You look as beautiful as ever this morning.

**EMMA**

Thank you, but I was up early already with Mulan.

**ERNST**

You are such a good mother. (*Ernst is giving Emma a hug.)*

**EMMA**

And you are a good father.

**ERNST**

Thanks. I was thinking of inviting my friend Atif and his family for a BBQ.

**EMMA**

That will be a good idea.

**ERNST**

Great.

***Next Scene***

*( Boaz and Helen are at a house on the beach at Musselburgh, Scotland. They are discussing events.)*

**BOAZ**

Rachel, what do you think we should do now? You fancy going to the beach?

**RACHEL**

Yeah, that will be good. It's a nice day.

**BOAZ**

I want to pray a bit and see where Jesus directs us next.

**RACHEL**

I will get ready.

***Next Scene***

*( Boaz and Rachel  are on Musselburgh beach. As Boaz starts praying Jesus appears to Him.)*

**JESUS**

Boaz, I have heard your prayer, and I have come to answer it. As My word says in Matthew 7:7, "Ask, and it will be given to you; seek, and you will find, knock, and it will be open to you."

As you see this sea before you, I have opened up the sea for Moses and the Israelites in the time that Pharaoh was chasing them. I delivered a miracle for them by opening the red sea, and when I closed it, the army of Pharaoh was buried in the sea with their chariots. The same I will do for My people again. My people are protected in this time of trouble.

I want you to go to Berlin, Germany, with Rachel and speak to My people who are there.

*(Jesus disappears.)*

***Next Scene***

*( Jachin and Suyin is still in Singapore. Jesus is speaking with Jachin in the middle of the night. Suyin is sleeping.)*

**JESUS**

Jachin, I have come to stir you so that you can awake My people. I want you to go with Suyin to The Doulos Phos Ship Hotel in Bintan, Indonesia.

I want you to speak from the ship's deck to the people. I am calling My people to come on My Ark. I am the Ark. Whoever comes under My shelter will be protected. Just as I have protected this boat to never sink and it was the longest on the sea, so I will do for My people.

This vessel was ordered on the 28th of August 1913, just more than a year after the Titanic sank. I want you to tell My people if they go the way of the world, they will sink with the New World System like the Titanic ship did, but if they follow Me, I have provided an escape for them. Go and tell them the good news.
*(Jesus disappears.)*

*Next Scene*

*(Boaz and Rachel are at The Brandenburg Gate in Berlin, Germany. Boaz is speaking. A crowd is gathering.)*

**BOAZ**

People of Berlin. Now is your time to change history. The strength of God's army is in people like you, who are resilient people. It's time to fight the good fight in the midst of the darkness of this world. It's time to shine bright and be a light in the darkness. Stand up for what's right, and don't be like sheep following this New World Order. God will give you victory! Gott wird dir den Sieg geben! Lob sei Gott!

**PEOPLE OUT OF THE CROWD**

Hallelujah!!

*(An army tank comes to disrupt the gathering. Boaz sees it coming. As it's coming close by, Boaz shows his fist in its direction. The tank is instantly thrown hundreds of yards backwards. People stand in awe. Boaz continues speaking to the crowd.)*

**BOAZ**

See, people, if we have faith like a mustard seed, we can even move mountains.
This army tank is nothing. Jesus said we would do even greater things than Him, because He has to go to His Father in heaven. Now is your time to do great exploits.

***Next Scene***

*( Jachin is with Suyin on the deck of The Doulos Phos Ship Hotel at Bintan, Indonesia. He is talking to the people on the deck of the ship.)*

**JACHIN**

Good evening ladies and gentlemen. I greet you in the name of Jesus our Saviour, the true captain of our destiny. Whoever believes in Him will not perish but have Eternal life in Him. He is the way forward, the truth and the life. He is the Gateway to our Father in heaven.

***("Our Father" song plays by Don Moon.)***

*(The people on the deck are kneeling down and worshipping God. The manager of the hotel ship is approaching Jachin. The manager has a ship's captain hat on. He greets Jachin and Suyin. He is also a Christian.)*

**HOTEL MANAGER**

Good evening Sir and Madam. I heard your message. I am also a Christian. You can speak freely here. Whoever is a friend of Jesus is a friend of mine.

*(Jachin and Suyin are shaking hands with the manager.)*

**JACHIN**

That's good to know, Sir.

**HOTEL MANAGER**

Yeah, I had a dream 5 years back where Jesus was speaking to me in the dream.

**JACHIN**

Tell me about your dream.

**HOTEL MANAGER**

I was on the deck of this hotel ship. I was standing where we are standing now.
Then suddenly, Jesus appeared to me.

**SUYIN**

What did Jesus say to you?

**HOTEL MANAGER**

He said to me; first, He loves me. Then He said He wanted to be Captain of this ship hotel.

**JACHIN**

What did you say?

**HOTEL MANAGER**

I said, of course, He can. He smiled at me and then disappeared.

**SUYIN**

That's a beautiful dream.

**HOTEL MANAGER**

So, you are welcome to speak to the guest on the hotel ship about Christ.

**JACHIN**

Thank you very much, Sir.

***Next Scene***

*(Boaz and Rachel are in Rome, Italy.)*

**BOAZ**

We are back in the Eternal City.

**RACHEL**

It somehow feels good to be back here.

**BOAZ**

I agree. It feels like this place will determine the end, also.

**RACHEL**

Yeah. Like you said to me before, both Paul, the chief apostle and Peter, the leader of the 12 disciples, died in this city. This city has a rich history.

**BOAZ**

On that note, we have to fulfil the mission of why we are here.

**RACHEL**

You mean going to the Vatican?

**BOAZ**

Exactly.

**RACHEL**

How are we going to get in there?

**BOAZ**

You know, that's not difficult for me. ( *Boaz is smiling.)*

***Next Scene***

*( Boaz and Rachel are at the main gate of Vatican City. The Swiss guards stop them from entering Vatican City. Rachel stays behind while Boaz walks through the doors. As the guards want to touch him, they fall down on the floor unconscious. He walks into the building towards the Vatican vault. The guards want to shoot him, but before they try, they pass out. Boaz takes the keys to the vault. He walks into the vault, and he takes stacks of gold and brings it out of the building. All the guards are still out on the floor.)*

**BOAZ**

This is enough for now. I will ask Jodhi to send a private plane to take this gold to Cape Town for God's People.

**RACHEL**

But doesn't this belong to the Vatican?

**BOAZ**

Have you ever heard of St. Lawrence?

**RACHEL**

Who was he?

**BOAZ**

He was a great Saint that safeguarded the Cup of Jesus of The Last Supper in time of Christian persecution. He was fighting for the poor. I tell you, if he was here right now, he would do exactly as I am doing.

**RACHEL**

Taking the Vatican's gold?

**BOAZ**

Yes, of course, to redistribute the gold of the Vatican to the poor.

***Next Scene***

*(Jodhi and Helen are visiting schools which they have opened up in Ethiopia. The children at the schools are flocking to them. )*

**JODHI**

You know Helen, since we started opening up more schools in Ethiopia, you can see the increase in pupils. It's phenomenal.

**HELEN**

Yeah, I just feel so privileged to be part of a happening like this.

**JODHI**

Yeah, it's truly by God's grace.

***(The song plays by Madonna "Like a prayer")***

**HELEN**

Since I have been with you, Jodhi, I have learned so much about the grace of God. Thank you.

**JODHI**

What do you mean?

**HELEN**

I always thought it was either right or wrong. It's either black or white.

**JODHI**

My love, if that was the case, there would have been only a very small crowd of people in heaven.

**HELEN**

Why?

**JODHI**

In God's house, there are many mansions. If God wanted to create robots, he would have done it.

**HELEN**

You mean like the world is doing now. They want us all to be robots.

**JODHI**

Yeah, that's right.

**HELEN**

So, the world is steering us in the direction of being perfect humans, but we will never be in this life.

**JODHI**

Yes, if God wanted us to be perfect, He would have designed us like that.

**HELEN**

So, what was our purpose given that He designed us the way we are?

**JODHI**

He wanted us to know what a family is.

**HELEN**

So, what is a family about?

**JODHI**

It's about unconditional love, like the Father in Heaven.

**HELEN**

Do you mean God is a family Himself?

**JODHI**

Exactly. Jessica always tells me she likes the number 3. It's God's perfect number.

**HELEN**

So, the number 3 resembles the Trinity of God, right?

**JODHI**

Yes. God, His Son Jesus and the Holy Spirit. They are our example of a perfect family in harmony.

**HELEN**

I get it. Joseph, who was the father of Jesus, resembles the Father. Jesus resembles the perfect Son, and the Holy Spirit is the One that connects us all in the Body of Christ.

**JODHI**

Yes indeed.

**HELEN**

So, Jesus had to die so that all families on earth could be perfect in the eyes of God.

**JODHI**

Yes. John 3:16 states, "For God so loved the world that He gave His only begotten Son, that whoever believes in Him should not perish but have everlasting life. He made reconciliation between God and man through the shedding of His blood for us."

**HELEN**

He wants all of us to be connected through His Son.

***(Lion King's Song "We Are One" is playing. )***

***Next Scene***

*(Ernst, Emma, Mulan and his friend Atif and his family at a BBQ at Ernst's place.)*

**ERNST**

My friend, so good to see you and your family again.

**ATIF**

I couldn't resist coming because your BBQs are always the best. Also, being right on the beach makes it the perfect venue.

**ERNST**

Thank you. Come, sit around the bonfire and relax.

*(They are all sitting around the fire. Atif's daughter is playing on the grass with little Mulan.)*

**ATIF**

How is it going with the airline?

**ERNST**

We are very busy considering the time we live in. As you know, the whole idea for the airline was for this purpose.

**ATIF**

Yeah, I remember clearly when you and Emma started the airline business.
It was the time you led me to the Lord.

**ERNST**

That was so great. Now you and your whole family are serving the Lord.

**ATIF**

Yeah, we are so thankful.

**ERNST**

Look at the beautiful sunset on Table Mountain.

*(They all look at the view.)*

**ATIF**

I told you we came here for the view and the BBQ and not because of you. (*They are laughing.)*

**ERNST**

I don't blame you. *(Ernst is smiling.)*

**EMMA**

Yeah, Ernst, that verse in Psalm 87:1 is so fitting now.

**ATIF**

What does it say?

**ERNST**

" His foundation is in the holy mountains."

**ATIF**

It sure is.

***Next Scene***

*( Jachin and Suyin are in North Korea. They are at Mansudae Assembly Hall in Pyongyang, North Korea. They try to see the Supreme Leader of North Korea.)*

**SUYIN**

How are we going to see the Supreme Leader without an appointment?

**JACHIN**

Leave it to God. For Him, it's no problem.

*(Jachin and Suyin are at the entrance door. Jachin is talking to the security guard.)*

**SECURITY GUARD**

Sir, who are you seeing here?

**JACHIN**

I am here to see the Supreme Leader.

**SECURITY GUARD**

Do you have an appointment with him?

**JACHIN**

No, but I have been trying to get an appointment with him for the last 6 months. His administration didn't answer my emails or calls.

**SECURITY GUARD**

Then you have no business being here.

**JACHIN**

I am sorry to say I have a specific message I have to deliver to him.

**SECURITY GUARD**

What message or whose message?

**JACHIN**

It's a message from the King of Kings?

**SECURITY GUARD**

What kingdom do you represent?

**JACHIN**

I represent the kingdom of God.

**SECURITY GUARD**

Where is His Kingdom?

**JACHIN**

His kingdom is everywhere.

**SECURITY GUARD**

Everywhere?

**JACHIN**

Yes, everywhere. He owns everything. The whole earth and the heavens.

**SECURITY GUARD**

Listen, Sir, I don't know your name, but if you don't leave here immediately, a whole army will be on you and your pretty girl.

**JACHIN**

Excuse me, Sir. She is not a pretty girl. She is a beautiful and strong woman. Next of all, she is my wife.

**SECURITY GUARD**

Right Sir. You think you are a joker. This is a very serious place. Now we will use violence.

*(The Security guard waves at one of the armed forces to get some troops.)*

**JACHIN**

Right Sir. I think you have just made a serious error of judgement. I didn't want to do this, but you gave me no option.

*(Jachin stretches his hand out, and all the troops, including the security guard, fall to the floor. Jachin and Suyin are walking to the Supreme Leader's office. They walk past the secretary into his office.)*

**SUPREME LEADER**

Who the hell are you?

**JACHIN**

My name is Jachin, and my wife's name is Suyin.

**SUPREME LEADER**

How did you come into this building? I have no appointments today.

**JACHIN**

We were nicely trying to get an appointment with you Sir, but no one would help us. So, therefore, we came by to see you by ourselves.

**SUPREME LEADER**

How did you get past the security guards and my troops?

**JACHIN**

Well, that was easy, Sir. If you have the help of God, nothing is impossible to do.

**SUPREME LEADER**

Why do you want to see me?

***( The song plays by BTS "Smooth like butter")***

**JACHIN**

I have a message for you from God. His message will cut like a knife through butter.

**SUPREME LEADER**

Butter? Why is God not speaking with me directly?

**JACHIN**

Yes, like butter. His sword cuts it smooth. He is speaking to you, but it seems that you don't hear Him.

**SUPREME LEADER**

Hey Clown, don't try to be smart here with me.

**JACHIN**

I am just the messenger delivering His message.

**SUPREME LEADER**

Listen here, clown face, you have one minute to tell me your message.

**JACHIN**

I only need a few seconds Sir.

**SUPREME LEADER**

Tell me.

**JACHIN**

God says let My people go. Set them free.

**SUPREME LEADER**

To go where?

**JACHIN**

To Southern Africa. We have tried to organise an airline to fly to your Pyongyang International Airport but to no avail.

**SUPREME LEADER**

What is the airline you are speaking about?

**JACHIN**

Saints 888 Airline.

**SUPREME LEADER**

The answer is no, so take your wife and get out of my face.

**JACHIN**

Sorry to hear that, but this is a final warning. There are always big consequences if one doesn't obey the Creator of the Universe. You would have to face that one day, maybe sooner than you think.

*(Jachin and Suyin are leaving the office.)*

***Next Scene***

*(Boaz and Rachel are at the White House. They have an appointment with the President of the United States. They are standing outside the White House.)*

**BOAZ**

So, this is what the White House looks like.

**RACHEL**

Strange, both of us are from America, but we have never been here at Washington DC, to see the Whitehouse before?

**BOAZ**

Yeah, as the saying goes. There is always a first time for everything. Ok, let's go inside and see. I like the idea of the Roosevelt Room. (*Boaz is smiling.)*

**RACHEL**

Ready, after you, my hero. (*Rachel is smiling.)*

*(A security guard meets them.)*

**SECURITY GUARD**

Sir, are you here for your appointment?

**BOAZ**

Yes, my friend.

**SECURITY GUARD**

I will take you to the secretary of the President.

**BOAZ**

Thank you.

*(Boaz and Rachel are going to the office of the secretary of the President.)*

**SECRETARY OF THE PRESIDENT**

Good morning. The President is ready for you. Let me take you through.

**BOAZ AND RACHEL**

Good morning.

*(Boaz and Rachel are entering the Oval Office.)*

*(The President is greeting them.)*

**PRESIDENT OF THE USA**

Good morning Sir. Such a privilege to meet 2 smiling faces in a time of real trouble. What is your beautiful wife's name?

**BOAZ**

It's an honour to meet you, President. I call her Wonder Woman, but her actual name is Rachel.

*(They all give a handshake.)*

**PRESIDENT OF THE USA**

Well, you two are doing special work in these times. No wonder you call her Wonder Woman. If she is Wonder Woman, you must be Captain America? (*They all are smiling.)*

**BOAZ**

It's a real honour to serve our country, Mr President.

**PRESIDENT OF THE USA**

Please sit down. Make yourself comfortable. We are going to have a nice chat.

**BOAZ**

Thank you, Sir.

**PRESIDENT OF THE USA**

So, I see you and your friend are turning this world upside down. (*The President is smiling.)*

**BOAZ**

Well, we try for the good, Sir. (*Boaz is smiling.)*

**PRESIDENT OF THE USA**

What is your friend's name again?

**BOAZ**

Jachin.

**PRESIDENT OF THE USA**

That's right. I saw it on the news. He doesn't take nonsense. He confused the Supreme Leader of North Korea. Good on him.

**BOAZ**

Yeah, he was trying to get an appointment with him, but they wouldn't give him one, so he had no other choice than to make sure he saw the Supreme Leader.

**PRESIDENT OF THE USA**

Unlike you. You got your appointment. (*The President is smiling.)*

**BOAZ**

Thank you, Mr President.

**PRESIDENT OF THE USA**

You are welcome. So, tell me, what is on your heart?

**BOAZ**

Mr President, as you know yourself, the USA has always played a pivotal role in world events for the good.

**PRESIDENT OF THE USA**

That's correct, and we always have acted out of our strong belief in God.

**BOAZ**

That's exactly why I am here.

**PRESIDENT OF THE USA**

Of course. I know you are a prophet, and that's why I listen to God's anointed men.

**BOAZ**

Yes, Mr President. You are like King David - he always listened to the prophets of God.

**PRESIDENT OF THE USA**

Thank you. So, tell me the message.

**BOAZ**

Well, you know the troubling times we live in, and the world is in havoc.

**PRESIDENT OF THE USA**

Yes, I know. Like never before.

**BOAZ**

So, God has prepared a place of safety in Southern Africa for the remnant of His people. We are here to help with that process, and we need your help to do it more efficiently.

**PRESIDENT OF THE USA**

That will be my privilege.

**BOAZ**

My friend Jodhi Livingstone and his friend Ernst are in charge of the Saints 888 Airline.

**PRESIDENT OF THE USA**

Yeah, I know that airline. A lot of my friends used it to immigrate to Southern Africa.

**BOAZ**

I am glad to hear that. Well, we are already using a lot of airports in the USA, but we want to use all of them so that we can accommodate all the people that want to go to Southern Africa.

**PRESIDENT OF THE USA**

That's not a problem. I will speak to a few people so that it will be done.

**BOAZ**

Thank you so much, Mr President.

**PRESIDENT OF THE USA**

No, thank you. I have read this morning in the Bible Exodus 14:14. So God is speaking to me too. (*The President is smiling.)*

**BOAZ**

That's amazing. It says, "The Lord will fight for you, and you shall hold your peace."

**PRESIDENT OF THE USA**

That's correct. Obviously, you know your Bible. You are Bibleman in the flesh. (*The President is smiling.)*

**BOAZ**

Thank you, Mr President. I want to tell you something about that scripture.

**PRESIDENT OF THE USA**

I am all ears.

**BOAZ**

You know that the Israelites were 430 years in Egypt before Moses delivered them.

**PRESIDENT OF THE USA**

I know they were there for many years but I didn't know it was 430 years. Any reason for that?

**BOAZ**

Yes, Sir, God works in numbers, and He does things accurately in His appointed times.

**PRESIDENT OF THE USA**

Tell me more.

**BOAZ**

Well, the number 43 stands for deliverance, and God used 10 plagues to deliver the Israelites, bringing them to a place of safety in the wilderness.

**PRESIDENT OF THE USA**

So, my maths is not that bad. You are saying 43 multiplied 10 times gives you 430. Bingo! Bible Bingo. (*The President is smiling.)*

**BOAZ**

Correct Mr President. There's more to the story.

**PRESIDENT OF THE USA**

Go on.

**BOAZ**

Well, you know that the first English settlement in Jamestown was in 1607.

**PRESIDENT OF THE USA**

Of course - the Pocahontas story.

**BOAZ**

Correct Sir. Do you know how many days it took the Virginia company to sail from London to Jamestown?

**PRESIDENT OF THE USA**

No Boaz. It seems to me you know our history better than I do. *(The President and Boaz are smiling.)*

**BOAZ**

It took 144 days.

**PRESIDENT OF THE USA**

I see where you are heading. I know that number from the Bible too. Doesn't the Book of Revelation speak about the 144,000 witnesses in the wilderness?

**BOAZ**

I see Mr President is sharp. (*Boaz is smiling.)*

**PRESIDENT OF THE USA**

Well, I hope so. Otherwise, the American people voted for the wrong man in this seat. (*They are laughing)*. So, tell me, what are the relation to the 144 days on the sea and the 144,000 witnesses?

**BOAZ**

You see, Mr President, God was planting a God-fearing nation on the soil of Northern America during that time. The Virginia company reached land for the first time on the 6th of April, 1607. It was Puerto Rico which is today part of the U.S.

**PRESIDENT OF THE USA**

Very interesting. Carry on.

**BOAZ**

Well, if we look at the calculation again, it's exactly 430 years from then to the date when The Great Tribulation started on the 6th of April, 2037.

**PRESIDENT OF THE USA**

Rachel, it seems to me that you have not only married this guy for his good looks, but he seems very clever to me. (*They are all smiling.)*

**RACHEL**

Yes, Mr President, he has the whole package. (*They are laughing.)*

**PRESIDENT OF THE USA**

It looks like it to me! So, Boaz, if I follow correctly, you are saying that now, after 430 years, God is delivering His people, to the wilderness, to a place of safety; again.

**BOAZ**

That's correct, Mr President. This time it's Africa!

***( The song plays "This time for Africa" by Shakira.)***

**PRESIDENT OF THE USA**

What about the 144,000 witnesses? What is that about?

**BOAZ**

Ok, my friend Jodhi in South Africa explained it quite well. The 144,000 refers to a remnant that is described in symbolic terms. The number "12" in the Bible is a symbol of authority. 12 tribes of Israel, 12 disciples etc. Therefore 12x12 = 144. The thousand represent the fullness of quantity. So, in short, it symbolises all God's people in this time that follow the Lamb, who is Jesus Christ.

**PRESIDENT OF THE USA**

It's all coming crystal clear to me now. One other thing. I have read about the 12 tribes in the Book of Revelation, but one thing that puzzled me was where is the Tribe of Dan?

**BOAZ**

That's a sharp observation, Mr President.

**PRESIDENT OF THE USA**

Surely you have the answer, a man of your calibre.

**BOAZ**

Well, I don't have the answers to everything, but I can give you my understanding.

**PRESIDENT OF THE USA**

Please do.

**BOAZ**

One has to go back to the beginning, which is the book of Genesis. The Alpha.

**PRESIDENT OF THE USA**

That sounds like a good start to me.

**BOAZ**

Ok, Mr President, I will read you the scripture. Let me Google it quickly.
*(Boaz gets on his phone to Google.)*

**PRESIDENT OF THE USA**

I like the world we live in. We don't have to carry Bibles anymore. We just get everything on Google. *(The President smiles.)*

**BOAZ**

Indeed. So, let's read. Genesis 49: 16-18

“ 16 Dan shall judge his people
As one of the tribes of Israel.
17 Dan shall be a serpent, by the way,
A viper by the path,
That bites the horse's heels
So that its rider shall fall backwards.
18 I have waited for your salvation, O Lord!”

**PRESIDENT OF THE USA**

Strict words for the tribe of Dan.

**BOAZ**

Yes, Mr President. But we also have to read what Moses prophesied over the tribe of Dan.

**PRESIDENT OF THE USA**

What did he say?

**BOAZ**

Let's read. Deuteronomy 33:22

22 And of Dan, he said:
“Dan *is* a lion's whelp;
He shall leap from Bashan.”

**PRESIDENT OF THE USA**

Where is Bashan?

**BOAZ**

This is the area that belongs to the Northern Tribes of Israel, but Syria wants to take it.

**PRESIDENT OF THE USA**

Is this what it is all about? Syria wants to take back this area?

**BOAZ**

Correct. That's why they broke the peace treaty.

**PRESIDENT OF THE USA**

Now I understand. That's all about the fight for the Golan heights.

**BOAZ**

Yes.

**PRESIDENT OF THE USA**

This goes back to the Yom Kippur War.

**BOAZ**

Yes, Mr President.

**PRESIDENT OF THE USA**

No wonder. That's the era of President Richard Nixon.

**BOAZ**

So, Mr President, God has chosen you to have your innings – to be a role player - for this appointed time in world history.

**PRESIDENT OF THE USA**

May I hit a home run by God's grace?

**BOAZ**

I am sure you will.

**PRESIDENT OF THE USA**

It was a pleasure meeting you guys. I have a few things to attend to now.

**BOAZ**

Thanks for your time Mr President and your airports.

*(Boaz and Rachel are greeting the President. They leave the office.)*

***Next Scene***

*(Boaz is calling Jachin. They are arranging to meet up in Tel Aviv.)*

**BOAZ**

Good Day Brother!

**JACHIN**

Boaz! Good to hear from you!

**BOAZ**

Same. I was thinking of meeting up with you guys in Israel.

**JACHIN**

Is it that time now?

**BOAZ**

I believe so, Brother.

**JACHIN**

Ok then, we will go. Shall we meet at the airport?

**BOAZ**

Yes, good idea. Let's meet up this weekend.

**JACHIN**

Hakuna Matata. *(Both chuckle and say their goodbyes)* No worries.

***Next Scene***

*( Boaz, Rachel, Jachin and Suyin are having a stroll on the beach of Jaffa in Israel.)*

**BOAZ**

It's good to be back.

**JACHIN**

Yes, a lot has happened since we were here last.

**RACHEL**

I would always love this place as it's the place I was born and grew up.

**SUYIN**

I know the feeling. One always feels at home when you are in the place you originally came from.

**BOAZ**

Well, we are nearing the end of our mission. One day, very soon, all His saints will live here in Israel.

**JACHIN**

Yes, but first we have to go to Jerusalem to fulfil our work there.

**BOAZ**

Yes, we have gone into the nations. I can feel the end is here.

**RACHEL**

When shall we go to Jerusalem?

**BOAZ**

Tomorrow morning.

***Next Scene***

*(It's the next day. Boaz, Rachel, Jachin and Suyin are at Solomon's porch in Jerusalem. A crowd has gathered together. Boaz and Jachin are speaking with the crowd.)*

**BOAZ**

Ladies and gentlemen, we are here to remind you that the end has now indeed come. This is the time that Jesus was speaking about in Matthew 24:29-31.

29 "Immediately after the tribulation of those days, the sun will be darkened, and the moon will not give its light; the stars will fall from heaven, and the powers of the heavens will be shaken.

30 Then the sign of the Son of Man will appear in heaven, and then all the tribes of the earth will mourn, and they will see the Son of Man coming on the clouds of heaven with power and great glory. 31 And He will send His angels with a great sound of a trumpet, and they will gather together His elect from the four winds, from one end of heaven to the other."

**JACHIN**

Boaz is right. We have prepared the way for the King of Kings, and He is about to return.

*(Guards of the Syrian army are coming to get hold of Boaz and Jachin.)*

**BOAZ**

*(Boaz is speaking to the Syrian soldiers.)*

You can try and kill us, but our time has not yet come to be killed.

*(As the soldiers try to approach Boaz and Jachin, fire comes down from heaven and destroys the soldiers. People stand in awe.)*

**JACHIN**

People of Jerusalem! Like this fire, God will destroy all the works of the enemy. No plans of the enemy can overturn the truth. Whoever calls on the name of the Lord will be saved, even in this hour.

**BOAZ**

Yes, the time has come to leave; the next time we see you again will be with Christ and whoever is worthy to be part of His Bride.

*(Boaz, Jachin, Rachel and Suyin are leaving Solomon's porch.)*

***Next Scene***

*(Boaz, Rachel, Jachin and Suyin are at Hyde Park London, speaking to a crowd there.)*

**BOAZ**

People of London, you have a great understanding of a kingdom.

**JACHIN**

Yes indeed. Boaz is correct in saying that, but it's time for the King of Kings to take His place and set up a new Kingdom that will last forever. We have fulfilled our mission to prepare for His everlasting Kingdom.

**BOAZ**

We say farewell, but just for a little while.
We will see each other again at His return for those who are worthy to be part of His People.

**JACHIN**

Farewell, not goodbye.

*(Boaz, Rachel, Jachin and Suyin are leaving the podium at Hyde Park.)*

***Next Scene***

*(Boaz, Rachel, Jachin and Suyin are at the last BBQ with Ernst, Emma, Mulan, Ann, Jodhi, Helen, Christian, Jessica and Helen's friend Stella.)*

***(The song plays "Time to say Goodbye "By Andrea Bocelli and Sarah Brightman.)***

**JODHI**

So great to have all of you together here. It's bittersweet because I know it will be our last meeting together.

**BOAZ**

As always, you are correct, Jodhi. It's been a journey, and you guys are friends for Eternity.

**HELEN**

It was a great journey but remember the last supper that Jesus had with His disciples. He said the next time that they will have a feast with Him will be at the Wedding supper.

**RACHEL**

That's correct, Helen, so we have a lot to look forward to. The best is yet to come.

**BOAZ**

That's correct, my Rachel. It will be our last time together. Destiny has its hand to play. God has planned something better for us in the next life.

**HELEN**

Boaz, you want to make us all cry now.

**BOAZ**

No, Helen, it's all good news. Remember, God ordains destiny. People talk about the Universe, but we know it is God. We have all eternity to enjoy it with our Creator.

**ERNST**

We are going too deep now. Let's celebrate the moment. (*Ernst is winking at them.)*

**JODHI**

I suggest we put the lamb on the fire. We are going to have a great night.

*( The sheep are going on the fire coals. They all sit around a bonfire next to the BBQ.)*

**HELEN**

So, let's make the night count. What do you want to drink?

**JODHI**

I have some good wine. Red or white, your choice. Also, we have some beer.

**HELEN**

I know my friend Stella likes Stella Artois. The beer with the Bethlehem star. So that's an option too.

**STELLA**

Thank you, Helen, for always thinking of me.

**HELEN**

You are welcome, my bestie.

**JACHIN**

As it's our last night together. Tell us something great, Boaz.

**BOAZ**

Well, greatness begins with God, as we all know.

**RACHEL**

Give us detail, Boaz.

**BOAZ**

You want detail. I will give you detail.

**SUYIN**

Don't make us cry, Boaz.

**BOAZ**

As it is said in the Bible:

"Those who sow tears
Shall reap in joy.
He who continually goes forth weeping,
Bearing seed for sowing,
Shall doubtless come again with rejoicing,
Bringing his sheaves with him."

**HELEN**

Boaz, what does that mean in pure English?

**BOAZ**

Well, to put it bluntly. Jachin and I are going to Rome to die.

*(They are all silent.)*

**JACHIN**

Sorry to break the silence, but there will be a resurrection.

**BOAZ**

Yeah, Jachin, let me tell them the whole story.

**JACHIN**

Ok, brother.

**BOAZ**

Well, my good friends, this is your last revelation from me. Next time Jesus will give you everything as it is.

**ERNST**

Tell us, Boaz.

**BOAZ**

So, as you all know, we are approaching the Day of Atonement. The Holiest day of the year on the Jewish Calendar.

**EMMA**

Excuse me for asking Boaz. What is the significance of that day?

BOAZ

I will explain.

JODHI

Please do.

BOAZ

The Day of Atonement or Yom Kippur is the most holy day of the Jewish calendar. In the Old Testament, the High Priest made an atoning sacrifice for the sins of the people on the Day of Atonement. This act of paying the penalty for sin brought reconciliation between the people and God.

HELEN

Is it still important today?

BOAZ

Yes, for sure. All prophecies in the Bible will be fulfilled.

EMMA

What still needs to be fulfilled before the Coming of the Lord?

BOAZ

The Day of Atonement and the Feast of Tabernacles.

ERNST

Ok, start with the first one.

BOAZ

A key part of the Day of Atonement at the Tabernacle and Temple was a sin offering involving two goats: They were chosen to be as similar as possible to one another; then they were brought before the

High Priest, and then lots were drawn, one bearing the words "To the Lord," the other, "To Azazel." The one on which the lot "To the Lord" fell was offered as a sacrifice. On the other, the High Priest confessed all of Israel's sins, and it was then taken away into the desert hills outside Jerusalem, where it plunged to its death.

**ANN**

Both were chosen to be sacrificed?

**BOAZ**

Yes.

**RACHEL**

So, Boaz, that is your and Jachin's destiny.

**BOAZ**

I am afraid so. But the good news is that we will be resurrected.

**ERNST**

Like the Book of Revelation says, after 3 and a half days.

**SUYIN**

That sounds very much like Jesus. He was resurrected after 3 days.

**BOAZ**

That's correct, and he also had a three-and-a-half-year ministry.

**ERNST**

That's very interesting. I get it now. The rapture of the Saints follows after that.

**BOAZ**

You have got it spot on, Ernst.

**RACHEL**

So that's where the Feast date of the Feast of Tabernacles gets fulfilled.

**BOAZ**

Correct.

**JACHIN**

That's pretty amazing – we will all see each other again on that day.

**EMMA**

That sounds great. It's a cataclysmic ending with an exciting new beginning.

**BOAZ**

Yes, that's how you should see it.

**ERNST**

Let me do the calculations. The Feast of Tabernacles starts the night of the $21^{st}$ of September.

**JACHIN**

Yes, on Sukkot. I think you should look at midnight at the start of the 22nd of September. Jesus gave us many clues in the gospel that the Groom comes at midnight.

**EMMA**

You mean like the Cinderella story.

**JACHIN**

Correct, His Bride is like Cinderella.

**RACHEL**

Just out of curiosity, do you think that will be on Israel time or Greenwich Mean Time? (*Rachel is smiling.)*

**BOAZ**

*(Boaz is smiling.*) I think Israel time as the Feast dates is all about Israel. (*Boaz is winking at Rachel.)*

**JODHI**

Boaz, what are your plans for tomorrow?

**BOAZ**

Jachin and I will go to Greenpoint Stadium and have a last message for the people before we go to Rome.

**JODHI**

We will all support you both there.

**EMMA**

I will get your flights booked for Rome.

**ERNST**

Yeah, we will take you to the airport, but for now, let's have a blast at our last braai (subtitles: Barbeque) together.

*(They enjoy the rest of the BBQ.)*

***Next Scene***

*It's the next morning, and Boaz and Jachin are speaking to the people of Cape Town at Greenpoint Stadium.*

**BOAZ**

Goeie, more people of Cape Town! (subtitles: Good morning, people of Cape Town!) We love you! Each time we came here it has always been a great blessing. Cape Town really feels like home for us.

**JACHIN**

Yeah, we will miss you, but the good news is we will see you all again soon. We always said this time of the end will come.
It is Boaz and my privilege to prepare you for the return of the King of Kings. So, on this note, be ready for His time has come.

**BOAZ**

Yeah, it's time for us to say goodbye. We are on our way to Rome. We greet you. Totsiens mense van Kaapstad. (subtitles: goodbye, people of Cape Town).

*(The crowd gives a standing ovation.)*

***(Song "Amigos Para Siempre" by Jose Carreras and Sarah Brightman plays.)***

*Next Scene*

*(Boaz and Jachin are at Jodhi's place and say goodbye to their wives.)*

**JODHI**

Guys, you have been such a blessing to us. There are no words for what you have meant to us.

*(Jodhi has tears in his eyes. He is hugging both Boaz and Jachin.)*

**BOAZ**

Yeah, it's not easy for us to say goodbye. We have to say goodbye to our dearest friends and our dearest wives.

**JACHIN**

It's been our pleasure serving you guys, and you have been such good friends to us.

**ERNST**

You have been a great inspiration to all of us. I suggest we give a group hug before you guys go.

*(They have a group hug, and then everyone is hugging each other.)*

**BOAZ**

May we ask you the last favour?

**JODHI**

Sure.

**BOAZ**

Can you please look after Rachel and Suyin for us? They are going to go through a hard time these few days, and there are no better hands to leave them in than you.

**JODHI**

Of course. We are all one family.

*(Boaz and Jachin are kissing their wives and giving them one last hug. Ernst and Emma are taking them to the airport.)*

*Next Scene*

*( Boaz and Jachin are at St Peter Basilica in Rome. It's the 10th of Tishri. They are speaking to a crowd of people.)*

**BOAZ**

We are here today at the Eternal City to give you one more message. It's a very simple message. Be ready for the return of Christ, which is at hand.

**JACHIN**

Yes, the time is up. Be alert to call upon Him in this last hour so that you can find Grace in His sight. Whoever calls upon the name of the Lord will be saved.

**BOAZ**

We are leaving you with the Peace of God. Take care because God cares.

**JACHIN**

Amen. Shalom.

*(Boaz and Jachin are leaving the square at St Peter Basilica. They are walking on the street Via Della Concilliazione, away from Saint Peter Basilica. Gunshots go off. Both Boaz and Jachin are shot. Their bodies lie in the street. The police come and let the crowd stand back from their bodies. )*

***Next Scene***

*(Ernst and Emma are sitting in front of their TV with Mulan playing on the floor. They see on the news Boaz and Jachin's bodies on the street in Rome. There is chaos, and people are screaming.)*

**ERNST**

Now I see. I always wondered how this would play out. Revelation 11:7 has just been fulfilled in front of our eyes.

**EMMA**

It's sad, but we know the end. It should make us full of hope.

*(Ernst gives Emma a hug.)*

**ERNST**

That's why I brought you here to the Cape of Good Hope.

**EMMA**

I am so glad you did.

**ERNST**

It was always going to be as if it was part of your destiny.

**EMMA**

I am so thankful for what God has planned for us. Look, we also have a beautiful daughter.

*(They are watching Mulan playing with her toys.)*

**ERNST**

Yeah, we are truly blessed.

**EMMA**

And, I think we did a good job with the Airline business for the Saints.

**ERNST**

You played a wonderful part in that. (*Ernst is kissing Emma.)*

*Next Scene*

*(Christian is going into the garden to call Jodhi to come and see the news of Boaz and Jachin lying in the street).*

**CHRISTIAN**

Dad comes and see the news. Boaz and Jachin are lying dead in the street in Rome.

*(Jodhi is running inside. Helen and Jessica also run after them to see the news for themselves.)*

**HELEN**

My word Jodhi. This is painful to watch.

**JODHI**

Yeah, it's strange Rachel and Suyin went for a walk. I don't think they know about this.

**HELEN**

Shall I call them?

**JODHI**

Maybe you better not. They will come soon anyway. We know the end of this story. They keep them lying there for 3 and a half days.

## *Next Scenes*

*(Scenes on TV where the people celebrate the death of Boaz and Jachin. They are sending each other presents and rejoice.)*

*(Emma is phoning Helen to see if the group can come together the next day at Ernst and Emma's place.)*

*(It's the next day, and the whole group is together. They are praying. It's a full moon, and they are sitting outside.)*

**ERNST**

Thanks, guys, for being here. I think it's important our prayers in this time.

**JODHI**

I agree, Ernst. We need to pray for the world. This is the last chance before the Rapture for people to say yes to Jesus.

**RACHEL**

Yes. The moon look's so beautiful tonight. It's the equinox, right?

**ANN**

Yes, it feels really special tonight.

**ERNST**

As we pray tonight, God will bring in a new time. He is the Bright Morning Star.

**EMMA**

Brilliant.

**JODHI**

Let's pray. (*They start praying.)*

*Next Scenes*

*(Jack and Johnny from the scene in Dallas, Texas, are sitting in a park. They have a discussion about how God has changed their lives in the Great Tribulation.)*

**JACK**

Johnny, I am so glad we came to our senses. The world is in a big mess, but we have given our lives to Jesus, so we are fine.

**JOHNNY**

Yeah, Jack, you were my drinking buddy a few years back, but we have come a long way since then. We have found our Saviour. We are ready for His return.

*(Jack and Johnny are shaking hands.)*

*(A scene in Rio De Janeiro, Brazil. Rodriquez and the waitress at the bar from a scene before in the movie are now married. They talk about what great things God has done in their lives.)*

**RODRIQUEZ**

I want to thank you, Salma, for what you have done in my life. When I came to the bar where you worked, I was so taken by you that I made it my regular bar.

**SALMA**

I know, but you were drunk every night, and football was your God.

**RODRIQUEZ**

I know, but you brought me to my senses, and when I gave my life to Jesus, everything fell into place. We even got married. Praise God!!

**SALMA**

Yes, it's because you made a definite turn and started obeying Jesus. See the reward He has given to you.

**RODRIQUEZ**

You mean He gave me you. (*Rodriquez is smiling.)*

**SALMA**

Of course. (*Salma kiss Rodriquez).*

*(Mr Chan, the billionaire who was in the Venetian Casino in Macau, China playing Black Jack, is with his family on Big Wave Beach in Hong Kong, where Jachin was praying for the rain to stop at the beginning of the Great Tribulation. He has given his life to Jesus. He is talking to his wife, Julia. They are talking about the Rapture too.)*

**MR CHAN**

Julia, thanks for all your prayers. For many years you have prayed for me, and I was not listening because I made Mammon my god. Thanks to your prayers, I awoke and became a born-again Christian. You saved our whole family.

*(Mr Chan is looking at his wife, and tears are rolling down his cheeks.)*

**JULIA**

I am just thankful that Jesus didn't give up on you. Now our whole family is ready for the Rapture of His Bride, and by God's grace, we are part of His Bride to be.

*(Their kids are coming. They have a family hug.)*

*(Bobby and Eric of Kingston, Jamaica, from a scene before, are at Lake Tania in Ethiopia. They are very happy and rejoice at being in Africa. They are both born-again Christians now. )*

**BOBBY**

Brother, aren't you glad that we have come to Africa? Bob Marley's song inspired us, and here we are.

**ERIC**

Yeah, we never expected that by coming here, that we would be saved. Today we are born-again Christians. Praise to God!!

**BOBBY**

Yeah, my mother was right; this was my destiny.

**ERIC**

Yeah, and the two witnesses you were talking about, well, you were right. They were untouchable.

**BOBBY**

Yeah, man, wait till you see how Jesus resurrects them. The world thinks they have won, but they don't understand that Jesus is the Resurrection of Life.

*Next Scene*

*(Jesus awakens the 2 witnesses.)*

***(The song plays "Swing Low" by Ella Eyre.)***

**JESUS**

Brothers, I am the Resurrection and the Life. I have come to resurrect you and take you home.

*(Boaz and Jachin come alive. The Holy Spirit awakens them. They stand on their feet.)*

**A VOICE FROM HEAVEN**

Come up here.

(*They ascend to heaven in a cloud, and the world sees them on CNN and on all the news channels all over the world.*

*(A great earthquake erupts in Rome. A tenth of the city's buildings fall down. Seven thousand people are killed. The people in Rome are in fear and give praise to God.)*

***Next Scene***

*(It's on the news the events in Rome. The group with Jodhi in South Africa is witnessing it. They thank God.*
*Jesus appears at Jodhi's house to all of them.)*

**JESUS**

I am the Resurrection and the Life. As I did with Boaz and Jachin, I will do to My Bride and take them Home. I am coming on the clouds with my angels to reap the harvest of the earth. I have sifted My people, and now My true followers I will bring to Myself.

I am sending out my angels with a great sound of a trumpet, and they shall gather together My chosen from the four winds, from one end of heaven to the other.

*(Jesus disappears.)*

***Next scenes***

*(The group are all at their own locations, sharing thoughts with each other before the Rapture.) First scene is Ernst with Emma and Mulan. They are giving a family hug.)*

**ERNST**

So, the time has come. We had a great journey together, and this is just the beginning of the next phase.

**EMMA**

Amen to that.

*Next Scene*

*(Rachel is talking with Suyin in the garden at Jodhi's house.)*

**SUYIN**

I still remember the day that we met at the Christian Conference in Singapore.

**RACHEL**

Me too. Look at what has happened in our lives. It was such an extraordinary journey.

**SUYIN**

Yeah, both of our husbands were such great characters.

**RACHEL**

Very true. They have fulfilled their purpose in life, and we will see them soon.

**SUYIN**

Exactly. (*They give each other a hug. Tears are flowing from their eyes. Ann is also arriving at Jodhi's house. She goes to the garden to meet Rachel and Suyin.)*

**SUYIN**

So glad to see you, friend.

**ANN**

Yeah, I thought the time was so near that I would spend it with you.

**RACHEL**

You are welcome. *(They all 3 hug each other.)*

***Next Scene***

*(Christian and Jessica are in the living room with Jodhi.)*

**JODHI**

I love you so much. You two have done great, and I am very proud of you.

**CHRISTIAN AND JESSICA**

Thanks, Dad. We love you too!!

**JODHI**

I am going to go for a walk on the beach with Helen. Will see you soon.

***Next Scene***

*(Jodhi and Helen are walking on the beach. They are holding hands. They are talking about their relationship and the Rapture.)*

**JODHI**

God has been really good to us. He gave you to me, and you are my lucky star.

***( The song plays of Madonna's "Lucky Star")***

**HELEN**

I hope I will always be your lucky star.

**JODHI**

You will be for Eternity.

**HELEN**

That's sweet. You will be my hero for Eternity.
*(They give each other a hug.)*

**JODHI**

Don't worry, Helen. This was a great life with you, but it's not the end.

*(Helen is putting her finger over Jodhi's lips to stop him from talking.)*

**HELEN**

I know what you are going to say. (*Jodhi is smiling).*

**JODHI**

You know me too well. Let's say it together.

**JODHI AND HELEN**

The best is yet to come.

*(A great sound of a trumpet is heard. Lighting, flashes, and thunder and hail happen on Bloubergstrand and Table Mountain, Cape Town.)*

***Next Scene***

*(Strand Beach, Cape Town. A woman standing on Church Street and seeing how people go into the Air. She is mumbling to herself about why she is left behind.)*

**WOMAN ON CHURCH STREET OVERLOOKING THE STRAND BEACH**

Why am I left behind?

*(A guy walks past her and answers her.)*

**MAN ON THE STREET**

It's because we were not ready.

*(Scenes in New York and Rome show how buildings fall down with great earthquakes.*
*Scene of the Acropolis in Athens on Fire.)*

***("The Mission soundtrack" by Ennio Morricone plays.)***

***Next scene***

*(Lightning comes from the East and flashes as far as the West, with Jesus on the clouds and the Bride of Christ going up from the 4 corners of the earth towards Him. A Scene on the Cover Page of the Rapture taking place from the Island of Guernsey, Channel Islands, UK.)*

# THE END

**SONGLIST :**

1) “Days of Elijah” by Robin Mark
2) “Exodus” by Bob Marley
3) “Don't worry about a thing” by Bob Marley
4) “ OMI – Cheerleader” by Felix Jaehn Remix
5) “We Are One Ole Ola” – 2014 Rio Football World cup song
6) “Money, Money, Money” by Abba
7) “Kingston Town “by UB40
8) “Summertime Chi “by Lee Foss, John Summit, Haley May
9) “Man in Black” by Johnny Cash
10) “It's time for the reign of God “by Brian Doerksen
11) “You're still the One “by Shania Twain
12) “Our Father “by Don Moon
13) “Like a Prayer “by Madonna
14) “We are One “a Lion King 2 Song
15) “Smooth like butter “by BTS
16) “This time for Africa “by Shakira
17) “Time to say Goodbye” by Andrea Bocelli and Sarah Brightman
18) “Amigos Para Siempre “ by Jose Carreras and Sarah Brightman
19) “Swing Low” by Ella Eyre.
20) “Lucky Star” by Madonna.
21) “The Mission soundtrack “ by Ennio Morricone.

Printed in Poland
by Amazon Fulfillment
Poland Sp. z o.o., Wrocław
10 March 2023

cafb90d5-260e-4616-95a8-d6fbaddd7c95R01